GUEST OF REALITY

This volume contains three texts by the Swedish author Pär Lagerkvist. The principal text is a new translation of his now classic *Guest of Reality* (1925), the previous English translation of 1936 having been long out of print. It is a novella, a work of fiction in which autobiographical material has been selected and ordered with the skill of a novelist. Set in a small town in south-east Sweden, it describes a series of episodes in each of which the boy Anders experiences a kind of epiphany. Through these episodes the reader gets a comprehensive sense of Anders' daily environment and of his bewilderment in the face of life's incomprehensible mysteries. The short story *Father and I*, from a collection published in 1924, is an encapsulation of many of the concerns amplified in *Guest of Reality* and is included here for this reason. *The Difficult Journey*, subtitled *Guest of Reality Part II*, appeared eleven years after Pär Lagerkvist's death in 1974. Now a young adult, Anders goes to Denmark and becomes involved in an intense affair with Hilde, an affair both liberating and crushing. *The Difficult Journey* is a compelling account of the overwhelming web of attraction and repulsion which can bind two people together.

PÄR LAGERKVIST

Pär Lagerkvist, an Immortal of the Swedish Academy from 1940 and Nobel Prize laureate of 1951, was born in 1891 in a small provincial town in southern Sweden. He lived abroad for years, in Denmark, Italy and France, where in 1913 the new Expressionist art profoundly influenced his thinking and his literary style, making him turn from naturalism towards powerful simplicity and the purity of expressionism. Of his nearly forty published books of poetry, plays, essays and fiction, *The Dwarf* (1944) was the first to gain him international fame, while *Barabbas* (1950) is perhaps the most widely known, having been made into a film by Dino de Laurentiis. Others that have appeared in English translation are *The Eternal Smile and Other Stories* (1954), *The Sybil* (1958), *The Death of Ahasuerus* (1962), *Pilgrim at Sea* (1964) and *The Holy Land* (1966). They centre around man's search for meaning, the problem of love and destructiveness, the enigma of man's soul. Lagerkvist died in 1974.

PÄR LAGERKVIST

Guest of Reality

Translated from the Swedish and
with an Introduction by
ROBIN FULTON

QUARTET ENCOUNTERS

Quartet Books London New York

First published in Great Britain by
Quartet Books Limited, 1989
A member of the Namara Group
27/29 Goodge Street, London W1P 1FD

First published by Albert Bonniers Förlag AB, Stockholm

British Library Cataloguing in Publication Data

Lagerkvist, Pär, *1891–1974*
Guest of reality.
I. Title II. Fulton, Robin
III Gäst hos verkligheten. *English.*
839.7'372 [F]

ISBN 0-7043-0079-6

Typeset by MC Typeset Ltd., Gillingham, Kent
Printed and bound in Great Britain by
The Camelot Press PLC, Southampton

CONTENTS

INTRODUCTION

In a notebook kept in the 1920s Pär Lagerkvist (1891–1974) commented on the very *non*-literary surroundings in which he grew up. He did so in a spirit not of resentment but of gratitude:

> I have had the good fortune and the privilege of growing up in a home where literature was not merely something unknown but also something which for religious reasons and despite its unfamiliarity was hated as a directly sinful and repugnant frivolity. At home there were no books other than the Bible, the Psalmbook and Arndt's *Sermons*.

A home where the word 'novel' represented something odious may seem an unpropitious environment for someone who in time became one of the major figures of twentieth-century Swedish literature – someone who in time was elected to the Swedish Academy (1940) and whose awards included the Bellman Prize (1945) and the Nobel Prize (1951). Yet looking back on his mother's fear of literature he could see it in a positive light;

> For my own part I can't see anything comical in this fear. On the contrary it seems to me to be something very serious and deeply interesting. These people had in fact no need of literature. It couldn't be used for passing the time, there was no time to pass. And through their deep religious sense and their strongly felt closeness to

> and absorption in real life, their existence was so rich they didn't need anything over and beyond.

In a word, daily life had an impact which literature can seldom provide.

In his youth, as could be expected, Lagerkvist felt exasperated by the pietistic small-town attitudes of his surroundings and he did his best to break away, both geographically (first Paris, then Copenhagen) and intellectually (critics have mentioned various turn-of-the-century trends, such as Darwinism and Social Democratic collectivism). But as is clear from his comments on the lack of literary stimulus in his background, his revolt against that background was by no means clear-cut. On the contrary, his memories of his early life, and in particular of the religious simplicities and certainties exemplified in his mother, and even more so in his grandparents, were to exercise a strong hold upon him throughout his life. As R.D. Spector put it:

> The quiet cathedral town of Växjö that stubbornly refused to yield its faith to the onslaught of *fin-de-siècle* forces, the pietistic religion of his parents' and grandparents' households – these nagged at his conscience, beckoned to him in his insecurities, and lured him with their simplicity. He had rejected the orthodoxy of his grandfather, who, when 'he heard the thunder rolling', could proclaim, 'It is good to know that the Lord reigns.' He had turned away from the farmhouse that rested secure in its faith of the single star that shone eternally overhead, and he had gone forth to wander beneath a maze of stars that attracted his intellect, but could not satisfy his soul. The past . . . remained a part of Lagerkvist throughout his adult life, shaping his personality and his work.

Guest of Reality (1925), which has established itself as one of the classics of modern Swedish literature, is in many ways an attempt on Lagerkvist's part to deal directly with his own early life and the community which formed it. Autobiographical elements are clear enough. Like the boy Anders, Lagerkvist himself grew up in a small town in

Småland, in south-east Sweden; his grandparents lived out in the countryside as peasants or small farmers, combining material poverty with spiritual certainty; his father worked on the railway and the large family (Pär was the youngest of seven) lived in a crowded apartment above the station restaurant. This restaurant is described in the first paragraph of the book – its architectural oddity, its bustle, its strange blend of dilapidation and festivity.

Yet if we are expecting a straightforward autobiography we may find Lagerkvist's manner of introducing his family curiously impersonal. The second paragraph begins: 'In the upper storey of this building an apartment had been fitted up, and here lived a family with many children.' And the main character, 'the youngest, Anders', does not appear until several pages later, and then almost incidentally. If we are looking for a continuous account of a young life we will find there are many gaps; clearly we are not being offered a matter-of-fact chronicle. And if we want to leave Anders at the end of the book on the threshold of adult life, then we may find the concluding page or so enigmatic and disillusioned.

The book, however, is not explicitly presented as autobiography – it is a novella, a work of fiction in which autobiographical material has been selected and ordered with the skill of a novelist. There is nothing here of the modern play between fiction and reality, and no question of creating fictional autobiography – what Lagerkvist gives us is a series of episodes based on his own childhood experience but presented in such a way that we can observe the boy Anders experiencing some kind of epiphany in each episode. As the book proceeds these cluster round each other to give us a comprehensive sense not only of the particularities of Anders' daily environment but also of his bafflement as he comes up against life's incomprehensible mysteries. It is not difficult to see a direct relationship between the awe felt by Anders in the face of questions apparently beyond the scope of his family's secure but narrow view of the universe, and the fascination with which Lagerkvist himself probed such enigmas in a lifetime's production of novels, stories, plays and poems.

This new translation of *Guest of Reality* replaces an

earlier English translation (from 1936) which has for long been out of print. This gives us the opportunity of printing beside it a short story called 'Father and I' from a collection published in 1924. Walking along the railway line at night, the boy and his father are surprised by the sudden onrush of an unscheduled train, and the boy experiences this as a foreshadowing of life, as a glimpse into an abyss, and the shock makes him sense that the secure world of his parents will not offer security for much longer. The closeness between this brief story and *Guest of Reality* has often been commented upon – indeed we can read it as encapsulating many of the concerns amplified in the larger work. In R.D. Spector's words: 'What is implied in "Father and I" is spelled out specifically, explored, examined, and evaluated in *Guest of Reality*.'

The third text in this book, *The Difficult Journey*, was not published in Swedish until Elin Lagerkvist's edition appeared in 1985, eleven years after Lagerkvist's death. The MS is dated 1925 and is subtitled *Guest of Reality Part II*. Now a young adult and in a state of mind which drives him to seek out situations full of tension and conflict, Anders goes to Denmark and becomes involved in an intense affair with Hilde, an affair both liberating and crushing and far from idyllic, in spite of the idyllic surroundings in both Denmark and Sweden in which it follows its rough course. 'Their love was like an instrument without strings. An instrument whose tone could have sounded full and deep, though perhaps dark. But the first thing they did when they met was pull the strings off it.'

The main part of the text (after a satiric account of a Danish boarding-house, which may have caused the author some qualms, for he was very attached to the Danes and their country) – the main part of the text is occupied first by an analysis of what Hilde's childhood must have been like, and then by a longer analysis of the stimulating tangle of attraction and repulsion which held Hilde and Anders together for a few months. The story as we have it ends with a description of a kind of epiphany experienced up in the snowy mountains, an episode abruptly ended ('they had begun to live again') by a clash which marked the end of their relationship.

Notes suggest that the piece might have ended with the return of Anders to his old home. But however the MS may have been completed, and in spite of Lagerkvist's claim that this second part was 'equivalent to' or 'on a par with' the first part, it is clear that this continuation, with its much narrower focus, would have been a different kind of book. Lagerkvist had nothing against its being published, but left the matter to his family.

Robin Fulton

Guest of Reality

Guest of Reality

In a small town in Sweden there was, as in all the other small towns, a station restaurant. It lay so close to the tracks that the smoke from the engines billowed along the façade and blackened it. The building would otherwise have been white, it looked as if it were meant to be some kind of dream castle, a complete little pageant; it was full of towers and pinnacles, little balconies no one could enter, carved embellishments everywhere, niches where there should have been urns with flowers, no end of empty flag-poles on the roofs. But it had turned out to be only a big building that looked rather desolate and was blackened by the smoke. Desolate however it wasn't and it even had something festive about it, travellers went there for a beer, they came and ate between the trains, and in the evenings music played in the back garden. It was castle which had been put to other purposes or which had become shabby because the festivities went on evenly and steadily, had no beginning and no end and no climax, the cork mats in the dining-room were worn, the plush sofas hollow seated and shiny after so many had sat on them, in the third-class café the floor was rough with protruding knots, the chairs unsteady, holed through, it didn't matter so much, it wasn't worth bothering about, the guests still arrived and anyway they'd soon be off again. They hadn't been invited to a sumptuous castle, nonetheless they sat there for a while, ate and drank while the trains stood waiting for them, shunting to and fro on the tracks, then the bell on the platform rang and the passengers went their way. It was never peaceful there, always people in a hurry, going somewhere else. But the castle remained with all its towers and pinnacles, its flag-poles and balconies, the empty niches, always with the same air of fairy-tale strangeness, drawing people to itself almost as if there were the prospect of a party.

In the upper storey of this building an apartment had been fitted up, and here lived a family with many children. Perhaps someone had thought of subdividing this part of the house into hotel rooms where travellers could spend the night, there would have been space for several in the long gloomy corridor, but nothing had come of this, they had made only two rooms and a kitchen, where the family had now lived for many years. At first the apartment was much too big, when the newlyweds arrived, but the children were born and grew up, more and more of them, and so it became too small. But they never thought of that, it was here they had their home and such things, by their way of thinking, couldn't be moved. The rooms were cramped and didn't get enough light, the three small narrow windows which each room had were high up under the ceiling, they had been designed for the sake of the outside, in order to look curious. The furniture was old and not so well made, it had clearly not been bought in town. The marks of the plane could be felt under the paint on the big brown bed and on the sofas where the children lay, these sofas had extensions and in the evenings they would fill a good part of the floor. In the good room there was a large round table with a crocheted cloth, there they ate on Sundays, otherwise in the kitchen. On one wall a picture representing Luther, on another an alphabet embroidered on canvas with many coils and embellishments and framed in glass. Above the bureau was a little shelf with an old worn Bible, Arndt's *Sermons* and two new Bibles which the oldest two girls had been given at their confirmation, these were covered with writing paper fixed on the inside with sealing wax. That, more or less, was what their home was like. Hand-made rag mats in many colours covered almost the entire floor surface and muffled everyone's footsteps. It was nearly always silent in there, although they were many.

Below the windows was a lean-to and this was the domain of the smallest children. They sat there hunched like baby birds looking out. Each had his own stool. Not really his own but inherited from one of the older children who no longer needed it. Every child has a stool, that's part of the order of things. But the children here had been given their stools so that they could sit up by the windows and look out. The trains went to and fro perpetually, shunted from one line to another, the engines whistled, pushed uncoupled carriages towards the station, the shuntmen ran along beside them waving their arms. There was always plenty to watch. Sometimes when the wind was blowing towards the house the smoke would sweep along the windows and if they were open there would be a great rush to close them. Then one could feel how silent it really was inside, the rumbling from outside sounded like something far away. But one still saw everything as before, the trains that stood for a time at the platform and then moved off and vanished with the white plate on the last carriage, the engines that were connected and disconnected as always. On the wooden bars of the windows lay a thin skin of soot which Mother wiped off, but it always came back again.

The stillness there at home was of a kind not often found in the world. Father came home for meals and now and then between meals too, he worked at the station and that's why they lived there. But Mother was always there, she saw to everything in the house and that never ended, there was always something and she never got out. She was fair with clear grey-blue eyes and her thin hair was parted in the middle. People can be fair in many ways, but she was one of those whose fairness was not only outwards, she was one of those we can feel came into being for the sake of that fairness, could live for it, nothing else could have helped her, given her enough support. Such people often seem fragile, as if it wouldn't take much to destroy them. If a strong rough hand swept over the world they would be wiped out, wouldn't be there any more. And the world would waken up from a good and beautiful dream and see only the hardest reality. But those very people have a strange sense of confidence and security, they walk around not like pale shadows but as substantially real beings, without cause for concern. It's as if they were quite certain they will not be wiped out, they will be there for ever, nothing bad will happen to them. They are as if they belonged to an old family that had lived through the ages, from the very beginning, despite change and destruction, so they have always been shielded, those who were easiest of all to break down. They have existed and will continue to exist as long as life endures. And the world will never properly waken out of its dream.

She was one of them. There was nothing unreal or remarkable about her, she was always seeing to things in the kitchen or in one of the rooms, chatting with the children, washing up, doing the laundry and the ironing, nothing special. When she didn't have anything immediate to attend to she would be darning socks, making clothes. While busy she was generally cheerful and she liked the bigger children to be joking about something so that she could go and listen, but if she sat down to rest she would clasp her hands on her knees and sigh heavily and seem to be far away from them. In the evening she sat reading the Bible or the psalter, not loudly, but whispering to herself. Then, by the lamp, she would look so pale and almost helpless, the small thin lips trembled. But there was nothing special about her, nothing else, for such as her it's enough.

When Father came home in the evening he pulled off his regulation tunic, blew out the signal lamp, dried it with a lump of cotton-waste and set it out in the corridor, for it burned train oil and gave off a heavy smell after being extinguished. Then for a time he wrote down wagon numbers and told them about which ones were to be loaded and unloaded tomorrow, mentioned this or that about the trains he had to attend to. But when they had eaten he would take the Bible down and settle to reading it. The atmosphere was strange and heavy when they both sat reading and no one said anything. The children kept quiet, it was so silent they felt oppressed. Below them was the third-class café and they could hear the hubbub and voices from the people drinking there. But that was something different and foreign which they didn't think about. Now and then when a late train came into the station Father would go over to the window, stretch, look out, his Bible still in his hand. Then he sat down again and went on reading.

The children were allowed to go out a little before bedtime, they crept along the dim corridor like a flock of rats and raised their voices only gradually as they climbed down the stairs. The spring evening was still light and it smelled as if it had rained. They crept through a little gate which led from the walled-in yard out to the park. Then the music could be heard, all sorts of instruments drumming, blowing, blaring, the flutes high and shrill, the trumpets raucous. There were lights burning further down the park. The children hurried in under the trees, made their way between the trunks, crept up as close as they dared. That was where several old spruces stood, their branches trailing on the ground; it was quite dark in there and the children crawled in, carefully, they mustn't get resin on their clothes. The open space in front of them streamed with light, it was packed with people sitting listening to the music, the fine folk had red rugs round their knees. The waitresses moved around among the guests and poured out marvellous drinks, one saw no more than their white blouses above the tables, they floated like doves. In the pavilion, which looked like half a house, the regimental band was playing, in shining uniforms. The roof above was a sky with stars of gold. The instruments glittered, the tunes rolled out in the quiet evening, towards the end of a piece the biggest brass instrument would start dripping.

The children stood breathless, with shining eyes, didn't dare move. It was all just as wonderful and beautiful every time, though they'd grown up with it.

When dusk fell, they crept back home and went to bed and dreamt of strange things they didn't understand.

But in the mornings an old tin churn with newly strained milk came in through the kitchen door. It came with a train which arrived at a quarter past seven and it stood beside the driver on the engine. The milk was still warm and had a smell of udders about it, the children drank as much as they could get. Stuck in by the lid was a note, wet from the splashing. It told of the spring sowing and the cows, whether anything had happened, or more likely that there was nothing special, they were well and everything was as it should be.

It came from the farm out in the country, that was where they belonged, where they came from.

The children would roam, noisily, in the park. It was so big it seemed like a whole forest, though a forest well ordered and tended. In one corner however it wasn't quite so orderly, the trees sprouted more or less anywhere and the grass was allowed to grow as it liked. That was their usual haunt, but they would wander a little here, there and everywhere. Up by the whitebeams on the mound next to the station yard and inside an abandoned spruce bower where a pile of sardine tins and broken glass lay in the middle, by the ant-heap not so far away, where the quaking-grass was knee-deep, as if the ants had manured it to hide their home from this world, and so over to the other side, where the lilacs blossomed along the edge of the long street that here marked the side of the park. The children were neither playing nor out walking, something between the two, at times they would take a hop or two, or follow each other between the bushes, then fall silent and listen to the twittering of the birds. It was an indescribably fine day. A few wisps of cloud lay resting up in the sky as safe as could be, the sunshine came unhindered down and tended the green things of the earth. One could well walk around feeling content with everything, as they did. The whole park was theirs, like this, in the middle of the day. An old fellow was raking the paths somewhere so far away it hardly concerned them, and anyway they knew him well so it didn't matter.

Perhaps they could hunt for lucky petals among the lilacs? Yes, they could. One of the girls always found some. As soon as she pulled down a branch and began searching through a cluster she would find several, both eights and tens. She was called Signe and more will be told of her later. When she came upon a really big one she'd become embarrassed, just because it always happened to be her. 'Oh no . . .' she'd exclaim, for she couldn't know if the others had found something as well. Then she'd clap her hands, burst out laughing and eat them up, that was what one must do if it was to have any effect.

Then they'd begin to play properly. The biggest boy would thump one of the girls on the back and run off and wait in ambush behind a tree. That was the start of hide-and-seek. They whirled around among the chestnuts and the maples, in between the elders where the earth wasn't broken up, so it didn't matter so much if they ran on it. This went on over the whole park, they were here, then there, sweaty and breathless, would crouch in a forked branch a little then run on, the girls must stop now and then and let themselves be taken, but when they'd got their breath back they were off again.

In the middle of all this they came right down to the outdoor café. They couldn't go further, but stopped, breathless, at the end of the pathways that led there, stood and looked, the game quite suspended. It was strange to see how altered and desolate everything now was in daylight. The tables stood empty and grubby, sticky with beer and punch that had dried in and now gave off a smell in the sun, under them lay countless matchsticks and chewed cigar stumps, in one place someone had spewed. The music pavilion gaped, empty and abandoned, the music stands shoved together like skeletons in a corner, bits of the starry sky had tumbled down. There was no joy and celebration here, no, by day they didn't bother about all this.

They got going again, picked up the game where they had left off, the one who was 'hit' chased the rest before him like a flock of sheep running wild and spreading into the bushes, the cries of distress from the girls peeled like despairing calls behind the trees, the flock whirled round the entire park from one end to the other hooting in the blazing sunlight.

But the youngest, Anders, didn't join in, and that didn't matter much either, for he couldn't run as fast as the others anyway. He stood on there looking in astonishment at the wilderness down in the café area, where in the evening everything was so indescribably beautiful. Now it was like nothing at all, only dirty and dreary. He couldn't understand it. He had thought it was all true. The sky and the stars, the streaming lights, the musicians who were like angels, and the music itself which sounded so sweet that there were times one didn't dare listen too closely. He remembered it all so vividly. And now – nothing left, nothing recognizable. How could something like that vanish and leave only emptiness and desolation?

He became frightened, felt such an oppression that his lungs could hardly breathe properly. And wasn't he standing shivering here, in the sunshine?

Sorrowfully he climbed up the path, looked down the slope. The cries of the others carried round the park but he didn't want to go over to where they were. Loitered about alone, didn't know what to do. Then sat himself down on the big broad path that cut across the middle of the park and had the greatest depth of gravel; on the other paths the gravel lay thinly over the soil for there hadn't been enough to go round. First he poured sand over his shoe and flattened it, and when he withdrew his foot there was a little cellar, to keep potatoes in or whatever, something that would keep. He made several, but it was quickly done, for he was good at it. So he set to digging a proper big hole. Clawed with his fingers, deeper and deeper, the sand became fine and wet, the hole at last so narrow his hand hardly fitted it. He was so engrossed he saw and heard nothing and didn't notice that the restaurant keeper was out walking nearby. Not before the man stood right over him and the shadow of the round paunch fell over his handiwork.

The restaurant keeper was a kindly fellew but the

children regarded him with awe for they thought he owned everything in the part of the world they occupied; in fact he didn't own very much and had only a ten-year lease which hadn't yet run out. He shook his head and fingered the watch-chain that lay in a wide curve across his waistcoat. 'No, that's not the thing to do.' And to be really friendly he added: 'When little children dig holes, it means someone in the house is going to die.'

To the other children he would have expressed himself more directly, but in the case of this one, who was so small, he thought he ought to explain the matter in some way.

Anders jumped up pale with fear. His face was quite rigid, he stared down in the hole, then threw himself trembling on his knees and filled it in.

The restaurant keeper thought he was behaving oddly and took a bag of caramels from his pocket, he liked children and more often than not he had with him something good for them. A caramel is always a caramel and Anders, with a trembling hand, took a big sticky one that was held out to him. But having nodded thanks he made off wildly, in among the bushes, over the lawns, up the park.

Who would die? Who would die? Mother perhaps? Maybe himself? No, he was too small, he couldn't die yet. But Mother – she looked so pale and sometimes said she felt tired. It can't be any of the waitresses they all looked so healthy and rosy-cheeked. No, it must be Mother, just think if it's Mother!

He fell in the grass, picked himself up and ran on.

No, it was Father! Yes, Father. He helped to shunt the trains – and he'll be run over! It was Father! Now he understood!

He ran on, to where the others were, he couldn't be alone, must find them! He wasn't able to hear them anywhere. Yes, they were up by the whitebeams. He scrambled up the slope, arrived among them pale and gasping, right into the arms of Signe.

The others didn't notice anything special, only that he came along as best as he could. Signe saw it at once and took him up. 'What's wrong?' she wondered.

He couldn't give an answer to that. Some things couldn't be spoken of, he had noticed, and it wouldn't have helped either, only made matters worse, one had to bear such things oneself as well as one could. But he clung fast to her.

The other children were clambering on to the fence and looking down into the railway yard. There was a steep drop beneath them where part of the hillside had been blasted away to make space for new tracks. 'Hullo!' shouted Helge, a bigger boy. 'There's Father!' Everyone must see – yes, there he was, standing on the step of the engine, holding on with one hand and waving to them with the other. Signe lifted up Anders, the smallest, as far as she could manage. Now Father jumped off and ran in under the buffers while the wagons were still in motion – Anders stared down in excitement. They couldn't see him, time passed. Signe felt the fingers clawing tightly at the side of her throat. At last he came out, signalled to the driver, and the wagons rolled into their side-track.

His sister set Anders down, he was shaking all over.

'That,' said the big boy who was leaning far out over the fence, 'was just where they should be. Johansson wants them there to load planks this afternoon. What'll we do now?' he went on, climbing down.

They stood conferring for a time.

'I'm going home to help Mother,' said Signe. And she took Anders by the hand to take him away.

So the two of them left the others. Down the lawns, past the bowling alley, which was rumbling like thunder. A fat man in shirt-sleeves came out and stood there breathing heavily with a glass in his hand. 'Bloody fine weather,' he said. 'Good-day, kids.'

They walked in silence, as if they weren't able to talk together about anything. Signe felt his hand still trembling but didn't know why. They came down under the trees, almost as far as the gateway into the yard.

Then his sister stopped. 'You can have this lucky one, Anders,' she said. And she looked for one she had kept aside, down in her pinafore pocket. It was a touch grubby and some cake crumbs had gathered on it, she blew on it so that it was clean again and opened out.

'No, you have it yourself,' he said.

'It doesn't matter, *you* take it. I find so many.'

He stuffed it in his mouth and carried on silently beside her, munching it down.

There was something special about Signe and Mother. It was immediately noticeable if one watched them about their household chores, which they did every day. In a sense they had a life together, one not quite like the others, superior in a way. They were like the heart which the others at home listened to in order to know for certain that they existed. One could sit listening to it in the kitchen, in the other rooms, wherever they went about seeing to things, whether they sat shelling peas in the garden, or washed up, or dusted, or polished knives on a Saturday afternoon. There was an intimacy between all in the family which held them together and separated them from the outer world, but that was nothing compared to what bound these two together. They were one, there was no distinction between them, only that the one wasn't as old as the other. It was something to be continued, not to come to an end, therefore the one was only a little girl and the other already a mother with many children, pale and worn, already past the middle of life. But they were at the same time two and one, and moved about talking together about this and that. Not that this made them solemn in any way, or that they said anything remarkable. No, that never happened.

Like today, for instance, as they work away at the washing in the kitchen. Nothing in itself, really, nothing special. They move round each other to pile up wrung-out clothes, change rinse-water, fetch the blue-bag, hang up stockings to dry outside the window, and in the meantime they say something now and then, laugh a little, then seize the washing-boards and turn serious again, both at once. Signe is a round little urchin figure who looks both funny and wise. She is yellow-haired, her head quite frizzy, her eyes sparkling. At the moment she is sweaty. She rubs the clothes so that the soapy water froths up, holds her head a little on the side as if to help her to push harder, her face is red with zeal, her hair glittering with tiny pearls of moisture.

'Oh no,' she says, breaking off abruptly. 'Just look.

It *has* fallen.'

'I've never seen the like,' says her mother. 'If only the dye hasn't . . .'

'Oh yes, Mother, it *has*. It's run on to the white. Oh dear what'll we do with this.'

'That was the worst it could do, Signe dear. It won't come? No – well, well. Nothing for it but try and boil it out. That's what we'll do.'

'Dear dear, that's the sort of mess we make. That's what I say . . .'

That's how they talked, about the things that cropped up. And then they'd bend their heads again over the washtubs, rinsing and wringing.

The whole house lay silent and desolate, one of those afternoons when it feels as if nothing will happen. Only up in the kitchen they were toiling to their utmost over the washing. The sun went in and out, shining or not shining on them, according to the little clouds that came and went up in the sky. The children were at school or away somewhere, each at his own ploy. 'But where's Anders?' Mother wondered. 'Probably sitting in by the window,' said Signe, 'since we're hearing nothing of him.'

He was. Sitting curled up on the projection and drawing with his finger in the soot on the window frame. When he finished with one section of the frame he would move to the next, the soot lay nice and thin everywhere. He didn't seem to notice the trains drawing past down in the yard. But he felt them, how they would glide and glide, changing and changing unceasingly. He didn't need to see. Only when one of them, on the narrowest track, near the windows, set off, he leaned out. It was much smaller than the others and looked so comical one couldn't help smiling. With a piping whistle it moved away and vanished into the birch-grove over to the right, puffing up little curls of white smoke above the tree tops. Of all the trains that passed he counted this one as his own and waved to it a little. Then sat down again to his soot.

So desolate and strange everything felt just now. The world seemed to have forgotten itself, seemed not to know what it was. This could be seen on the houses across the yard, on everything. The world was at a standstill, quite empty and deserted. – And he sat there drawing.

No he did not want to sit there any longer. Why not go down to the yard and try to find something to play with? It would be best if he did that, it would make a change.

He climbed down and walked through the rooms. Out in the corridor was the door to the kitchen, he stopped there, put his ear to the door and listened. Mother and Signe were talking in there, what they were saying couldn't be heard properly for they were scrubbing the clothes at the same time and the water was splashing in the tubs. It sounded like a peaceful murmur. No, he didn't want to go in. But he did want to stand out there and listen for a while. Now Mother was saying 'Signe, don't you think we could have a drop of coffee soon? We've certainly earned it.' 'I should say we have.' 'Put the pot on then, while I rinse out the towels.' 'Oh-h-h!' says Signe, 'it's good to straighten up a bit.' Then she laughs. And so the rings on the stove start rattling.

He crept away, down the gloomy stairway and out into the yard. There were buildings right round it. The sun was scorching at the moment but he didn't seem to notice. In one gutter the dishwater had mounted up because corks and lemon rinds had blocked the grating, he went and looked at that. Alongside stood a pail where a bunch of withered carnations lay at one with coffee grounds and ash. He went round the outhouses. On the one side were four doors leading to the privies. Away in a corner was a big stack of boxes with empty beer bottles, smelling of the dregs. From there he crossed to the opposite row of sheds, but took a detour to avoid coming close to an unpainted building which had been put up in the middle of the yard. He would prefer not to recognize its existence. It had no windows, only a black hole in one wall, if you put your hand to it a shiver ran through your whole body. For the shed was full of ice. No, he'd rather go and look into the woodsheds. The doors to all three stood open to let the firewood dry, there was a scent of birch as if he had stuck his head into a forest. In the furthest away of the three forests a little old man stood sawing. He had a big white beard, yellow with snuff under his nose, and small peering eyes. Apart from that one didn't see much of him in the half twilight.

'Good-day, young shrimp,' he muttered. 'What are you up to?'

'Nothing,' said the boy

'Well well, I can just think so. But old Jonsson's sawing his logs. He's been doing that since he wasn't bigger than you. Morning to evening, day after day, till he became as old as he is now. Look how old he is. And all this drudgery just so people won't freeze to death. How many do you think would have frozen to death if old Jonsson hadn't stood here sawing his logs all his life? Thousands, I can tell you. Your father and your mother and Signe and the restaurant boss and all the waitress hussies – the lot would have been dead of cold, winters and winters ago. But no one thinks of that. Has anyone come and *thanked* me they're not dead? Not one. They don't think that's anything to say thank you for. But one fine day old Jonsson'll be fed up, too tired and old, and can't be bothered standing here slaving for them any longer. And *then* they'll freeze to death, all of them. Don't you think it'll serve them right?'

Anders only stood there, restlessly, staring in at him.

'Yes, yes, that's how it'll go for them anyway. It's dreadful cold here in the world if there aren't fires, that I can tell you.'

'And look you,' he went on, 'don't stand there looking so down in the mouth about it all. Out in the sun with you, boy, make sure you keep warm while it's summer, then we'll see how things are when it's winter.' And strangely enough, he broke into a broad smile.

The boy did as he said, stepped out into the world and looked around. At the moment there was no lack of sun, the grass between the cobblestones stood shining, and along the gutter, where the spaces between the stones were richer, slender dandelions stuck up. It was peaceful as a Sunday. If only he could understand why he had to feel so oppressed. It was like a weight on his chest. Should he perhaps creep up and listen at the kitchen door again? No, he'd rather be down here, it was a beautiful day, one ought to be out, being glad in some way. How could he manage that? He wanted to, went as far as the big gate and stuck his head out. There was a sandy square in the sun and then a hawthorn hedge and above, summer clouds that didn't move. But otherwise there was nothing, only air, and up in the air it looked totally empty, as it does at times. He drew his head in again.

Perhaps after all he could just as well climb up into the ice-house? That was perhaps the best thing to do anyway. Yes, that was best, he must do that.

He crawled up the plank that lay steeply from the ground up to the hole in the wall, kept a rigid hold on himself so as not to fall down. He daren't look up towards the black hole but tucked his head in, crawled like a crab with his fingers round the edges of the plank. The chill streaming out could now be felt on the back of his neck, now he was level with the opening. Jumped in as fast as he could, without looking.

It was pitch dark inside. He groped over the wet sawdust, his whole body shivering with the cold. The ice block wasn't level, more had been cut away in some places than others, so there were holes here and there, and here and there the ice had piled up. Round the edges the ice stuck out uncovered and made his fingers quite stiff.

He crept round in there, in a state of excitement, felt how cold, how dreadful it was. His heart thumped – no, he wasn't freezing, his temples were throbbing as if he had a fever. It was terrifying. It was like being buried, not knowing if one were alive or dead. It made one shake with terror. . .

Who was that walking down in the yard, it sounded like Father. . . He crept forward to the opening, looked carefully down. Yes, it was Father arriving home. He wanted to call to him, go with him up to the kitchen, hold his hand up the stairs, he certainly didn't want to be here – no, it was best he stayed here, it was surely best. Father disappeared into the vestibule, he stood watching him with an open mouth but without calling.

How cold and horrible it was. Always the same darkness and icy cold. He crawled further in, the cold felt even colder. His shoes sank in the wet sawdust, along the walls and up on the ceiling the dampness dripped. He stood still and let himself, in a way, stiffen. Didn't move a hand, not a finger. Was as if gone.

No – how long had he stood like this? He didn't recognize himself. Was he frost-bitten? No, his head, his whole body, burned. He was too feverish – he must get across to the opening, breathe the proper air and look down into the yard. Panting, he stood there and looked out, clung on tight with his fingers, his head barely above the edge, his eyes hot and scared.

Then Father came out again with a basket in his hand.

'Father!' he called, loudly, he thought, but what came was little more than a gasp. Hardly audible down there. 'Father!' he shouted again. This time Father looked up

'Goodness, what're you doing there? Come on down! What are you up to? We've been looking for you, don't you want to come along to Grandmother's, I'm taking the trolley.'

'To Grandmother!' exclaimed the boy, waving his arms. 'Wait, I'm coming, I'm coming now!' And he pushed himself down the plank with hands and feet, as fast as he could.

Rushed over to Father, clung to his arm, hard.

'Which trolley,' he gasped, 'the station master's or Karlsson's. We're going now aren't we, what's in the basket, is that for Grandmother, what's that, we *are* going now, right away – ?' He spoke non-stop, vehemently.

'What's wrong?' asked Father, looking at him. 'What were you doing up there?'

'Nothing,' he replied, and glanced down. 'I only stood inside a little. . . I wanted to go out with you. We're going now, aren't we, now?'

'Come on, child, come on,' said Father, taking him by the hand. They went out through the gate, out on to the sandy square, in the sun. The little boy was breathing heavily but gradually became calmer. He looked around, up in the sky, down in the sand that lay glaring, yellow and newly raked in the sunshine, at the hawthorn hedge so full of blossom it was almost white. So, when they had walked a bit, he looked up at Father in a tentative way and tugged his arm. 'It'll be great out driving,' he said and laughed a little shyly. 'Oh yes, it'll be fine,' said Father. Then, a few steps further Anders took a jump to himself. Ran ahead and opened the gate into the railway yard, clattered halfway down the steps and then back up to keep Father company, out among the tracks and walking on the rails, on them and off them, now to and now fro. 'You're in a fine mood, aren't you?' said Father. 'Yes it's a nice day, isn't it? Watch me run on the rails!' 'Watch you don't fall!' Father shouted after him. But he didn't fall. Soon he was back again. 'Where'll we find the trolley?' 'Yes, yes, we'll soon see, it's over there in the goods shed.'

They were soon there. The entire contraption was tilted up against the wall, a three-wheeler and a long pole to punt it along with, that was all, no miracles. First they had to content themselves with walking behind it and pushing, only the basket could sit on it. 'Can't we start soon?' wondered Anders. 'Oh yes,' said Father, 'just wait till we get past the points.' Anders was off ahead to see that the points were open the right way, so that the trolley wouldn't tip over with Grandmother's coffee and sugar and the bit of yeast lying on top of the basket. Lifted the wheels if they stuck. At free moments he jumped along beside the trolley.

Out here along one whole side of the station yard lay the town cemetery with graves right up to the railway lines. He didn't care to think about that, looked the other way instead. It was rather long, the cemetery followed them all the way out. Still, he had the basket and the trolley to look after, and the piles of planks at the other side to watch. And of course he could talk to Father, the time went quickly. Now he knew that they had come so far that there were no longer any graves, only some newly planted limes on a lawn that was waiting for those who were going to die, who still lived. He crept closer to Father. 'Can't we start soon?' he whispered. 'Oh yes, just a little patience, child, just a little.'

Almost immediately, out past the gates, they set off. Anders sat crosswise, his feet towards the little wheel, hung on tight to both the basket and himself. Father stood on the long side between the two big wheels and handled the pole.

They soon gathered speed. In no time at all they were right outside the town. The pole gripped firmly and evenly in the gravel, the wheels span as fast as they could, over the joints they went tickety-tack just like a real train. It was a windless day yet the wind blowing over them made them pull their caps over their ears. 'Holding tight?' Father yelled down, crouching to gain speed. 'Yes!' he yelled back and looked up and laughed.

First there was a straight stretch over the meadowland. The flowers whirled past like dots, one couldn't see what kind they were, up towards the embankment wafted a scent of all of them together. And then they drove into the forest. A sharp scent of spruce came in the airflow and a fine delicate aroma of birch, still quite recognizable, and of juniper and elm and pine, it was mixed forest, a bit of everything. Then a touch of wild strawberry scent for they passed several strawberry patches along the top of the embankment, they shone so red one could still see them long after they were gone, but on they went, always past, on they went. Down the bank were flowers of every possible kind, ox-eye daisies, birdsfoot trefoil, buttercups, cow-wheat, little tufts of clover that had strayed here, wild oats, raspberry thickets and many more. Scents and bright colours glimmered for a moment and rushed past, the spruces and the birches and the junipers down in the forest as well. The telephone poles hurried away back as if they ran home, didn't want to come with them.

Anders sat with staring eyes, taking in everything, his cheeks were a little pale from the rushing air but he was hot with excitement and elation, his heart thumped and thumped. He was in a sort of ecstasy. Father heaved himself forward and backward to get a good leverage. He had to watch that the pole didn't strike the sleepers, for then it would slip, but this was a precaution he took by habit and their speed got better and better.

Here the line curves to avoid water-courses. There is water everywhere, lakes, rivers, streams, ponds. In the middle they came to a little bit of bridge, where a stream had to pass. There Father made an extra effort, there was a rumble and they were across. 'Don't lose your hat!' he shouted down to the boy. 'No-o-o!' shouted Anders back and clung to his cap, the basket and everything. The pace was headlong.

Now they shot past the Näs linesman's place, his children looked out from among the lilacs in amazement, clenched their pinafores and curtseyed. Immediately, they reached the big bridge over the river, where they had to pole themselves forward pushing on the sleepers with the wide current roaring underneath. And so they reached Näs station.

Here they checked their speed a little, but not much for it was a small station with only two sets of points, one at each end. The station master was out walking up and down in front of his premises. He saluted as if to a proper train, one of those that don't stop at small stations like this.

Then they picked up their former speed again. The line passed ploughed acres and clover fields, open land belonging to a biggish farm but not looked after very well, and so into the forest again. Deciduous trees this time, they stood shimmering in the sunlight on both sides, full of birdsong. Eight men were here, working on the line, replacing decayed sleepers. They got a brief rest while the trolley rushed past, greetings to be exchanged despite the speed, but raising one's cap was more than one dared. Anders had to return greetings just like his father, but with his head to the side so that he could hang on to the basket too.

Then a gradual rise, but at the speed they had it was hardly felt. From the top of the rise the line slopes right down through the open countryside, it's called The Street and you travel there for nothing, free, just swish along. At the highest point there's another linesman's cottage. The linesman himself was up by the chimney tarring his roof in the glare of the sun. 'What sort of extra-special's this!' he shouted down at them. 'That's just what we are!' Father yelled into the wind, for already they were speeding off down the slope.

Father drew in the pole, held it ready to use as a brake on one of the wheels if necessary. The air whistled round their ears. The little wheel at Anders' feet span so fast the spokes were invisible, it hopped and skipped with joy. It was like a young foal in the morning just when it's been set free. The rail was a straight line, ox-eye daisies, buttercups, cowslips also became straight lines, the telephone wires glittered tautly up against the sun, the sparrows sitting on them suddenly scattered in terror into the forest where trees and bushes grew together into a smooth wall, a squirrel, startled out of its wits, scampered up the fence as if it couldn't get through.

It was over in a few minutes, all of the long slope. Then the countryside opened around them in every direction, with marshlands, little lakes, all sorts of waters, with tilled strips, grazing lands, countless ploughed squares, with fenced pastures, boglands and woodlands and farmsteads scattered among the oats and the rye out in the sun. The light was so friendly and open everything could be seen, and in the distance Grandfather's place was in sight, sheltered in a group of maples. The speed slackened.

They rolled peacefully over a broad river edged with reeds and water-lily pads, in the current they could see shoals of bleak stirring in the glitter. Finally they reached a bumpy track that crossed the line, where they braked and jumped off and there they were, they'd arrived.

'That went fine!' laughed the little boy as he marched about beating his arms. Father smiled contentedly, heaved the trolley down into the grass beside the track. Then they went through the gate and set off over the fields with the basket between them.

Anders was so exhilarated he could hardly use his legs properly. Father was also light-headed and walked as easily as a twenty-year-old. To cheer him up still more the boy would jerk the basket a little, then they'd both laugh from the sheer joy of being out and walking here together.

There was something strange about Father. He was really meant to be happy. But that was seldom apparent, only like this now and then, there was usually something inside him that was too heavy. He couldn't free himself of it and he always went about serious and at times as if oppressed. He had many cares, but it wasn't that. He was just made that way, and the melancholy part of his being held him back, as if it were something unjust. His joyfulness was in a way subdued by his seriousness.

But now they were happy and exhilarated, both of them. The familiar property lay on both sides with all its greenery in high-summer splendour, the rye smoking, the air trembling above the grey fences because they were hot. Their road took then away from the river, they walked past the mill and the miller stepped out big and floury, just in time to greet them. Over a stream, then up a low hillock, then they had the farmstead just below them.

The house was tall, with a narrow gable, the dark red paint had almost worn off, so that the grey timber showed through. The maples grew above the roof, which was of delicate old moss full of quaking-grass. The outhouse lay on the other side of the road and was old, except for one part where it had been extended.

They hurried along as fast as they could, kept looking to see if someone was waving by the curtain. There was no one to be seen, but a calf came bounding to meet them, stretched out its wrinkled neck over the fence, muzzled their fingers and mooed. That made the curtain stir. And now they were there, making their way up the garden.

It was full of apple trees, pear trees, lilacs and, furthest in, big flowerbeds, peonies, dahlias, marigolds in bright colours, tall hollyhocks, geraniums which had been set outside because it was summer, stock, lavender and mignonette spreading their scent far and wide. Along the path went a low hedge, Anders walked on tiptoe to see over it into the currant bush. But there was Grandmother on the porch step, in the midst of all her flowers. 'Dear children, so it's you!' she greeted them. She was so old that she called both of them children. Anders knew of nothing so remarkably old. Her face was thin and worn, not wrinkled yet full of furrows, her body short and strong, in a skirt grey and dry as earth. Nonetheless she was very like mother. The eyes were the same, the hair just as thin, though hers was white. There was the same fragile lightness about her, though she looked so stern. She took their hands, thanked them for all the coffee and sugar that the boy must show at once. And so she pushed them in through the door and came behind them in her knitted socks.

Inside there was a strange smell of old wood and of earth and of dried manure that hung by the clogs in the porch. And from a room upstairs there penetrated the smell of onions which lay spread out on yellowed paper.

They lifted the latch and stepped into the big living-room.

It seemed quite gloomy at first, coming in from the outside. Two big beds with covers on them and a big table in the middle made up most of the furniture, by the window stood a loom with linen for sheets. In the open fireplace a huge copper cauldron hung, for they were boiling potatoes for the pigs. There sat Grandfather, minding the fire. He was powerful though aged. His face large and broad, smoothly shaved, the mouth strict and toothless. His hair was long and white and reached down to his shoulders. He was wearing moleskin trousers and a leather waistcoat with lead buttons. Didn't move, for he was stiff in the legs, let them come over to him.

'How's Grandfather?' greeted Father. 'God be praised,' said the old man in the raised voice of those whose hearing is dull. 'I lack nothing. How is everyone there in town?' 'Fine thank you we are in good health,' Father replied loudly and clearly. 'And you, little one, did you get to come with Father on such a long journey?' The old man took the boy on his knee and ran a big veined hand over him. Anders always thought it strange sitting there with Grandfather, looked at his rough face, clung on to the waistcoat, it was almost too stiff to get a grip on.

Father and Grandfather sat talking together for a long time, loud and slow, so that the cottage resounded. The old man wanted to know about something or other. Everything was treated in the same serious tone. If they happened to mention something pleasant, that too was discussed solemnly, as if it weighed them down. Father had changed. He sat with clasped hands, his back stooped a little, looked older, just as he did when he sat reading the Scriptures at home in the evenings. The smell of the potatoes spread through the room, the windows steamed over.

Grandmother crept to and fro between the kitchen and the room. She could never rest, always must have something to do and so her work was never finished. She went about in socks so as not to be heard.

Now she came and tried the potatoes, they weren't ready yet. 'But now, child, what about going out to the currant bushes!' she said to Anders. And he woke up, realized it couldn't be right for him to sit in here with such old people, climbed down and stole carefully out.

The brightness of all the flowers almost stung his eyes at first, especially the peonies, which shone like flames everywhere. The sun was beating against the wall and the flowers were wide open for the bees that scrambled in and out, for exquisite butterflies that merely nudged them, as if they lived off scents. He crept down into the currant bushes. There was warm fine earth underneath, the hens had been there scraping around, making little piles as if to lay eggs in, preening off a few feathers. He pushed aside some of these dry remnants and sat down in a suitably large dent, reached up into the bushes and ate. The bunches hung all round him. Some were bigger and more bitter because they had been hanging in the shade, those in the sun were small and sweet, so one could pick and choose according to how they tasted. He plucked carefully and with consideration, for he wanted to eat for a long time.

Crouching in here he was out of sight and sound. And there was no one to see or hear him anyway, no one in the garden and no one on the road, it was peaceful and quiet. Only away out on the marshland by the river a cow would moo now and then, and beside him under the currant bush a few flies would whirr. That was all. No wind that could be noticed, the maples stood asleep in the sun, even the aspen, normally a restless tree, stood still not far behind him by the southern gable. Sometimes he'd push aside a twig and look up, to rest himself in the sky between the bunches and on some cloud that stopped there, unable to travel further today.

Just as he had eaten his fill Grandmother appeared on the step on her way to the pigs with the potatoes. She looked and listened for him, he could see, though not to much purpose. 'Where are you keeping house, boy?' she called. 'Don't you want to come and feed the pigs?' But he crawled silently under the bushes so that he jumped at her down by the gate instead and gave her a little fright. If it had been dark she would have been properly frightened, but it wasn't. They went down together into the outhouse.

The sow lay seething in the sty with piglets at all her teats. She hung down in the muck even when she rose, but the mountain of flesh was grunting with pleasure and the little pigs tumbled off her in every direction. She slurped in the contents of the trough at one go, the piglets also tried to get at it but couldn't reach up. Grandmother and the boy went to see to some other things in the outhouse. It had to be mucked out after the oxen, and a cow was being kept inside for it was about to calve. The hatches to the dung heap had to be opened. There was a shortage of manure here in the summer because it all went to waste in the pasture, there was hardly more than a puddle that the sun glittered in. The cow turned heavily in its stall and mooed as it looked out through the opening. A hen up on the loft boards cackled shrilly. 'She must have laid,' said the old woman. 'Go and look, Anders!' And he clambered up the ladder.

He stayed up there in the darkness for a little, to flop around in the hay that smelled so good. It had just been brought in so it was loose and one could fall about anyhow. It was dark here but that didn't matter. The light came in only through a little opening, he went across and had a look out, hung there a while, dangling his legs. He found the egg and then one more in another fluffy pile. 'Mother can have these,' said Grandmother.

It was good coming here with her, doing odd jobs and chatting on and off. She was serious and prudent but so mild that that was hardly noticeable. It was just like with Mother. And while with her one seemed to see everything very clearly, and that gave one a special secure feeling.

When they were finished inside it was time to go out to the pasture to milk the cows before evening came on. The afternoon was fading though the sun still shone warmly. The grass was wet so they walked barefoot, Anders followed Grandmother's big feet over the tussocks, her feet looked so old and they had thick corny patches caused by her wooden clogs. The cows came towards them and let themselves be milked quite submissively, but Anders had to hold their tails to prevent them splashing about, the flies wouldn't leave them in peace.

Out here people were not well off, but it was beautiful, one could see far up into the parish along the course of the river that flowed through it. The land lay at rest and the farmsteads had long shadows stretching towards the river. It was, on the whole, low-lying, yet with a variety of pastures, gentle wooded slopes and ploughed strips. Down here in the lowest part, the ground scarcely seemed to rise above the level of the river-bed and in the marshes there were black holes where the sunlit water was hectic with water beetles and suchlike. It was a proper summer's day, the smallest insects were happy.

As they turned homewards with the milk there was a rumble low in the west and the air felt a little sultry. Uncle, who ran the farm, had come back from the forest with firewood and was driving in the oxen. It was nice to meet him. He was blue-eyed and fair, middle-aged, stocky and strongly built, but he looked as if he had worked hard. When he shook hands his skin felt as stiff as bark, he had lost a finger at a wedding once, when firing a salute. They helped him unyoke the oxen and drive them into their stall. Uncle was very quiet this evening, perhaps tired, his tiredness could be heard from his breathing as is often the case with people who do heavy work.

All three of them came up through the garden together. The thunder rumbled again and the air became oppressive. How the weather could turn out like this no one understood, all day it had been nothing but fine. Father and Grandfather were still sitting in the cottage, resting in the gloom. It was supper time for all.

The old lady blew more life into the fire and set on a frying pan with pork cutlets. Took out plates, set the table. The men talked. The wind rose in the maples out in the garden and it darkened further in the house. Grandmother put the pan on the table, on two slabs of wood, the pork was sizzling and smelled good; then the old man himself got up, said grace in a loud voice, solemnly, and as if weighed down by his words they all took their seats, helped themselves and ate.

As they ate they said nothing. The old woman sat somewhat apart, at the other end of the table, now and then crept out into the dark kitchen and came padding back again. The flash of lightning lit up the room. They looked up and sat waiting, the rumble came from far off. 'We shouldn't have the fire on,' said the old lady. 'It's far away,' answered Uncle and took another helping. The trees shook again outside, where it was so silent each leaf could be heard. The hollyhocks knocked against the glass, then the windows flared again. The rumbling was heavier. Immediately there was another flash.

'I'd better be getting home,' said Father, who was on duty that evening.

'Hope you don't get caught in the storm,' murmured the old woman.

'Can't be helped. Anyway, I may miss it. Anders should perhaps stay overnight, we'll come back and fetch him in the morning.'

To the little boy it was strange he should be

separated from his father. Stay on here alone – did he really want to? Here it no longer felt as it had done only a little while ago. He'd rather go home. No, not worth the risk, they decided.

They finished their meal and Father said goodbye. Anders watched him step from the one to the other, followed him with his eyes. Then accompanied him into the porch, stood watching him. The garden lay in a desolate gloom. The tall maples were grey because the leaves were blown back by the wind. And there was Father – vanishing up beyond the rise! It felt so odd. Would he ever see him again?

A violent flash illuminated the whole landscape, far out across the marshes, the heathery slopes and the ploughed fields – the earth looked quite grey and dead, the sky flared. He plunged into the house, the outer door was blown shut behind him, he butted open the door into the room and rushed in, stiff and pale with fright. Then the roar came, crashing from all sides, the window-panes rattled. The old man by the fire raised his head, looked around, out through the window. 'It's good to hear the thunder,' he said, 'we know God rules!'

Then he got to his feet stiffly and slowly and went to fetch his Bible. 'Where's my brush, Stina?' he said. The old lady found it for him, a little round homemade horsehair brush with a handle of coiled twine. He groomed himself until his hair lay white and splendid down to his shoulders. Then he undid the clasps on the big Bible, opened it, and began to read:

> Hear and give ear; be not proud, for the Lord has spoken. Give glory to the Lord your God, before he

cause darkness, and before your feet stumble upon the dark mountains, and, while ye look for light, he turn it into the shadow of death, and make it gross darkness.

He raised his voice even more as he read, each word rang clear and loud in the room. The old woman padded around listening, crouched and small, stopped and sighed heavily. Uncle sat by the window looking out. The whole room flared with lightning, the trees were lit up clearly, and the explosion fell almost at once. The old man didn't budge, went on reading.

Grandmother had cleared up and now took a chair and sat down to listen better. No one moved. The flashes struck between the windows, and now the rain came, streaming down the panes, the thunder pealed unbroken, the storm was right overhead.

The boy shifted about in the room, sat crouched by the loom, crept out and sat by the table, then away in the corner by one of the beds, all according to how he thought the lightning would strike. The others sat still and listened. He didn't take his eyes off the old man. The furrowed face was unmoving, the forehead was almost smooth, but in the cheeks and round the mouth the furrows cut in deeply, as if he had been harrowed by a long life. The truth indeed is that in his manhood he had been rather unruly, but there was no need to talk about that and Anders knew nothing of it. But throughout his youth and ever since he began to grow old his aim in life had been to fear God and let himself be guided in God's way. He had a tranquillity that nothing could disturb.

The thunder began to pass over, could be heard

further and further away. He went on reading. The old woman sat and watched him with clasped hands, following his mouth.

The rain stopped, only the trees could be heard outside. The clock on the wall struck nine. Then he closed the book and looked upwards. 'Amen, in the name of God Almighty, Amen.'

Anders crept forward. It was bedtime now. Uncle, who slept in the little room upstairs, said goodnight and went up. The little boy was left alone with his grandparents, who were so old, he was to lie with them. It felt strange. They undressed, he had to help the old man pull his trousers off his stiff legs. At the bedside the old man fell on his knees and uttered the evening prayer in a resounding voice, the old woman had to help him up again, so they both lay down to rest, with a sheepskin over them so as not to feel cold, though it was summer.

Anders was soon ready, crept into the other bed. It was so big he filled next to nothing of it, the cover lay stiff right up to his chin, weighed him down as he breathed.

With wide-open eyes he lay staring up into the darkness in an effort to sleep. It was dark everywhere, out in the garden, down by the river, far out on the marshes, and darkest of all in here where he lay alone with both the old ones. He listened – nothing to be heard. They must be asleep now. The maples couldn't be heard either, none of the trees anywhere. But most silent of all was in here. Only his heart thumping.

He thought of Grandmother and Grandfather lying over there, how old they were. They were quite wrinkled with being so old. And they had an old smell, different from his – he felt he could sense it over here. Everything here had a smell. The straw in the bed where he lay, the rough ticking. The sheep's wool in a pile under the loom. The broad worn planks of the floor with black filling in the gaps. The soot in the open fireplace that gaped out into the room. The earth that clung to the wooden clogs out in the porch. Everything had an old smell. Everything was terribly old.

Couldn't he sleep? His heart went on thumping. He felt he couldn't breathe, the cover weighed upon his chest. He was hot all over . . .

Ssh! . . . No, it was nothing.

Why didn't the old ones hear how they drew breath! *He* heard all too clearly how he panted . . .

Could he really not hear them? No, it was quite silent!

Were they dead? *Perhaps they were dead!* They were so old, so near the end, the end could come any moment. *Perhaps they were dead!* He must get up. Up in the darkness. *They were dead.* Groped forward . . . across the floor . . . up to the bed . . . Held out his hand . . . felt Grandfather . . . the wrinkled neck . . . the gaping mouth . . .

No, they were both sleeping safe and sound.

He crept back, into his own bed. Tiredness got the better of him and he fell asleep. Now and then he turned restlessly, sighed deeply. He dreamt it was dark, everywhere, in the garden, far out on the marshes, in the forest, in the railway yard, over Father and Mother, everywhere. And the darkness was a big grave where all the dead lay along with all those who were still alive. And above in the flaming sky a huge thunderous voice read out incomprehensible words over the living and the dead.

When Anders was twelve he found himself one autumn day on the way out to a stone he had in the forest outside town. It was rainy and windy, without being stormy, as it often is in autumn. He kept to the railway line since, as they lived beside it, that was the natural way to take into the forest. It was grey and chilly. In the marshalling yard he saw his father walking about taking a note of the wagons, a little stooped and with his back wet from the rain. He stole past on the other side of the row of wagons so as not to be seen by his father, who would well wonder where Anders was going in that weather. He heard his father's step when they were opposite each other, he himself walked as silently as possible so as not to be heard.

Strictly speaking he hadn't thought he'd need to go out there today, but that's how it had turned out anyway. He hadn't remembered this, had been preoccupied with other things. Also, the day had been beautiful for a time, and he didn't usually go out there in good weather. But later he had decided after all to come, had realized it would be best.

The rain was streaming down, but he didn't walk quickly. Solemnly, and as if dejected, with his hands stuck down in his pockets, in a tight little jacket with yellow buttons. An engine was busy shunting, gave out a pleasant warmth in passing.

Yes, in the morning it had been properly clear, even if raw. He had been up early, by six, because the sailors came on the train, fifty boys off down to the naval station out by the coast. They stopped for coffee, and on the square in front of the station restaurant long trestle-tables had been set. They shouted and bellowed with their mouths full of rolls, the coffee steamed and spread its scent in the chill of the morning. And they waved to the children up there in the small windows, no doubt thought it comical to see them stuck up there. Took snuff and piled back into the train.

News of this had come the evening before, so they knew they could get up early to watch. Then he had slept a little more and so to school. In the morning break he had to see to his homework and fetch paraffin for mother. He hadn't thought of that earlier. He never thought of such things until they were necessary. The weather changed, became as it was now. After school he had helped Gustav carry garden chairs down from the outdoor café area, they were to be taken in for the winter, stacked up in the bowling alley, which was now closed. Gustav bowled a shot and made the skittles clatter down for the last time this season. Then Anders had gone home on his own. Stood and listened a while outside the kitchen door because Mother and Signe were sitting talking quietly about something in there, thought it was about his being ill, perhaps not likely to live much longer, he had been listening to that now for about a year, though he couldn't feel there was anything wrong with him. Sat up by the window and watched the trains shunting to and fro in the rain. Then he'd realized he must be out to the stone today. For it was a heavy day. He felt compelled, no doubt about that. He had to follow his compulsion.

By now he was passing the depot out at the edge of the station compound. An engine was there, loading up with coal, it too gave out some warmth as he walked past. But then he was out on the line, open land on both sides, and the rain came driving with the wind, up over the high embankment, uneven and whining, it was blowing with a vengeance. He held his head down and braced himself when the gusts came. It was worst here. But it *should* be hard. It should be like a sacrifice.

That . . . that they talked about quietly, could it perhaps be something different? But what? Occasionally he'd noticed how he'd heard wrongly, that they hadn't actually been talking at all, only sitting in silence. But today, quite definitely, they'd been sitting there whispering. Why were they talking quietly, if it weren't that they thought he was going to die soon? Otherwise they could well have talked loudly.

In the greyness the wind howled over the fields, the sky drooped low. Now he was entering the forest and the air calmed a little, now it was only raining. The water dripped from the trees, the spruces trailed their branches, couldn't be bothered holding them up for they were full of dampness. From up here on the embankment one could look down into the forest. He carried on, it wasn't so long now. Drops were running on the telephone wires, but they were going in the other direction, towards town. He stepped on the sleepers, they were tarred, didn't take in the wetness, it just lay in pearls over them.

Now he was there, climbed down from the track, through the fence and into the forest. As he pushed his way in through the trees the rain cascaded off them. Because of the bad weather it was already almost dark in here, it certainly wasn't late. A little way in, surrounded by tussocks, lay a flat stone which was barely a few inches above ground level. There was nothing special about it. If anything was remarkable it was simply that there was a stone here at all, there were no others, the mossy earth let them sink. He glanced carefully round, out along the track, though no one would be likely to come that way. And he lay down on the stone and prayed.

It was silent all around him, only the dripping in the trees. He was not to be heard either, he didn't pray out loud, but his cheeks were burning. Straight ahead there was a swampy opening in the forest and in the middle stood a stunted pine, barely the size of a man, uneven and stunted. He looked at this all the time, though it wasn't to it he prayed, only that this was what he always did. No, he was praying to the same God as they did at home, there was no difference. But he did it out here. Why, he didn't know, it had just turned out that way. It wasn't for the sake of prayer out in nature – nature was nothing solemn for him, on the contrary. But still. Praying at home was no use to him, it wasn't eager enough, not worked-up or fervid enough for his prayers to be heard. To be sure of being heard demanded much. Therefore there wasn't much point in coming here either on days when the weather was good, when it was nice to go out walking. Then he may as well not try. He didn't really know – it was exhausting and strange, this need to come out here, it often plagued him. But then it ought to be hard. It had to be so.

He had his own way to follow. He lived in a world of his own making, a narrow world with tenets and prescriptions which were not to be disturbed, not to be acted against, he went around like someone in a cellar in the daytime, groping forward. Nothing could be done about that. It *was* so.

His cheeks were burning hotter and hotter. He lay with his hands tightly clasped. But he was praying for no more than one thing:

That he shouldn't die, that none of them should die, none of them! That Father should live, and Mother, and all the children – he counted them all – and the old people out in the country, all, all of them! That no one should die! That things should stay as they are. That nothing should be changed!

His whole passion for life amounted to this, that it shouldn't stop. He asked for no advantages beyond that. Only to live. Things can turn out as they like. That wouldn't matter. That couldn't be helped.

He was indeed insistent on that – life could be whatever it chose, he insisted, to show how little that mattered. In this way he could be so much more certain of getting what he asked for, that which meant everything. He half dozed, *thought* exactly about what he named, so that he really *saw* it, he sort of held it forward. Prayed and prayed that it should be as it was, that it shouldn't end. That winter should come soon, that summer should come round again in summer-time, that life should go on, go on – and that he and all the others should be there too.

He lay there enflaming himself into an ecstasy, more and more glowing and hot, so that he was quite filled by it. It sounded like a hymn to life within him, a strange hymn which didn't become any kind of jubilant song, but only counted up everything, only held on desperately to everything. Yet still a hymn.

In the glade before him the rain poured down, drenching the greyish-yellow moss and the tree he stared at. But in here it was quite silent, dim as evening. It was solemn in its own way, as he lay there praying on the stone in the half darkness. He didn't stir, not even his mouth moved. Only the glowing cheeks and the fingers he pressed together as hard as he could.

After his praying he rose quickly. Relieved, as if glad it was done, dried off his wet knees.

Jumped over on to a tussock, and then to another. He knew his way around here, but it was very wet today. At least he could walk on the tussocks. The spruce twigs hung full of rain that lay in pearly drops between the needles, the elms stood with smooth shiny branches, on the small birches there were still a few leaves left in sheltered corners, they made the bushes look like big yellow flames, in the heather and the moss there were also fiery colours.

How beautiful to live, if only for a while. He wouldn't die now at once, not today, not tomorrow either. No, not now when he had just prayed to live. The birches and the low sprigs of cowberries, the fine blossoming heather, all greeted him: Good-day, little man, you're alive and walking about here. What are you up to?

He leaped around on the tussocks like a fledgling. Looked up into the trees, thought he heard something, perhaps squirrels? Shook a spruce branch and let the water splash down on the cowberries, shook some more down on some berries he would come back and pluck some day. And so he climbed back up to the railway line.

He moved more rapidly now. The drops up on the telephone wires ran in the same direction, they were going homewards too. He looked around, up to the treetops and the clouds in the sky. The weather had lightened noticeably, pigeons were cooing in the forest, other birds were beginning to chirp and twitter.

He reached out a hand. Was it really raining still? No, it wasn't. The sky spread itself unevenly and thinly as if it could open whenever the time came. Sparrows appeared on the wires, sat shaking the rain off.

Yes, the world was . . . however it wanted to be. One way or the other, it wasn't to be counted upon. It pleased itself. Not much point in having special wishes, as far as the world went, that was clear. So long as one could be alive, take part in it. And that's what he was doing.

He went on. Passed the edge of the forest, where there were two cellar-like sheds where the ironmongers in town kept gunpowder and dynamite, thought what a bang it would make if it blew up. Came out into open country, the wind was no longer so terrible, from the embankment there was a clear view in every direction. Came to the depots and into the station. Shunting here and there, engines whistling and puffing out smoke, the two narrow-guage locos peeped pitifully like baby birds, spat and frothed round their cylinders as they pushed together carriages for the evening trains, the big proper engines on the wide-guage track billowed their smoke up to heaven in a more dignified manner. Shuntmen hung out from guards' vans and goods wagons in motion, flapped and signalled with their arms. One engine had five flat open trucks with boxes of cowberries. Another came puffing along with a long line of bellowing cow-trucks. It was lively here. He stepped forward carefully between the trains, stepped over the tracks when it was safe to do so, greeted firemen and drivers, shuntmen and brakeboys on their way with lanterns down to the trains. Thought about this and that, felt very happy.

Where had he got all that from? All that about dying. He wasn't going to die! No more than the others. Not till much later, and that went for everyone. They just had to put up with it like that.

Now it was over and done with, for this time, his heart felt light, he was back again, among the others. People were walking up and down the platform carrying bags, old women came rushing, imagining they'd be late. Olsson rang the first bell, Karlsson drove out the luggage, hooted at people in his way, The fireman lit the lanterns at the front of the engine ready for the journey out into the world.

He climbed up the restaurant stairway, home to his own place. From the third-class café came brawling noises from a couple of drunks the train was about to leave behind. But already inside the yard with all the woodsheds it was silent. He crept up the steps, along the dim passage. Outside the kitchen door he stopped and listened a little – no, no one was whispering in there. He hung his jacket up here in the darkness, for it was wet, and he crept in.

Mother was there, making supper. They talked a little. He gathered that she thought he had been up in the park for a time. On his part he was lively and happy, talked about the sailors that morning and about Gustav's last shot in the bowling alley before it was closed for the season. Mother moved about surrounded by the light she always spread around her, calm and quiet. He thought she was so serious.

Then in came Father, and all the other children, and they ate. The lamp was lit in the room and Father and Mother sat down at the table and read God's Word, while the sisters made the beds, silent, whispering, they were hardly audible. He sat curled up by the window, it started raining again, beating against the window out of the dark. The last trains hooted and drove off with the glare of their fires showing up against the sky. But in here it was quite silent and motionless. Only mother sighing now and then and her lips trembling as she read. It all made one so oppressed, it was as if she needed help, as if she were alone.

How heavy everything was for everyone here at home.

One morning the milk-churn didn't come alone. Grandmother stepped off the train, carrying it, she was dressed in her Sunday best, in her old fine kerchief. She clambered over the tracks, looking cautiously about her, and walked up to the restaurant where the waitresses were hanging about the windows watching for customers. She curtseyed to those she met. Here in town she seemed even smaller. Her dress was black but the greyness in its folds was caused by age not by use. The skirt reached down over her feet, hiding them, and was so stiff it hardly moved as she walked. Her silk kerchief was a wedding present, it had roses pressed into the fabric. It was so big she almost vanished in it, the fringes fell down over her shoulders, and above the knot her old firm chin protruded. Instead of a coat she had a brown shawl wrapped round her waist and knotted behind. It was winter, frosty and clear, slippy underfoot. She walked lightly for her age, only a little stiffly because of the shawl. Looked up at the towers and pinnacles on the house, the snow-filled niches and balconies –

no one to be seen in the little windows above the third-class café. Still, she wasn't expected. At the gateway lay a snowdrift from overnight, she had to step over it. In the yard, where there was a smell of beer, she curtseyed to the restaurant-keeper and Gustav, who were shovelling snow, went into the porch and so up. When she knocked on the kitchen door it was the youngest one who opened. They were washing themselves, getting ready for school. Mother was there, cooking porridge. No, no one knew anything about her coming. 'God bless you, my children,' she said and sat down, a little tired. 'I've come with the milk. At the right time too, I see you're going to have your porridge.' Mother helped her off with her shawl, the old lady seemed so small in the chair, the woollen waistband tight and creased against her breast. Her kerchief came off too, the thin white hair shone, and so did the good eyes, that lay deeply inset as they do with old people. Yes, she brought greetings from them out there. All was well with them, God be praised. Uncle Emil was in and out of the forest a great deal, with the oxen, he had a struggle of it, poor man, things just don't go so quickly when you don't have a horse. Grandfather was fit and well. And the cows were milking well, they still had plenty of feed left. Yes, God was good to them all. Next week they were going to slaughter the pig, they'd already said so in a note that came with the milk the day before yesterday.

But why had Grandmother come to town like this without their knowing about it?

Well, *they* thought she should come. She was against the idea for she thought it wasn't really necessary. It was just that she'd been feeling a little out of sorts recently, nothing to speak of, but still they thought she should perhaps see what the doctor said. It was their idea, not that it was necessary.

Mother sat close to her and took her hand, everyone fell silent. Everyone looked at her. They thought she was just as usual. Well, possibly a little more shrunken. And perhaps thin in the face? But then she always had been. The eyes lay so remarkably deep. But that's how they were with old people. Yes, they thought she looked as she always did.

But Mother sat and patted her, asked just what was the matter, where she felt sore. Oh well, it was just that she felt a little poorly and got quickly tired at her work, so it went rather slowly. But she had no pains, nothing to speak of, well perhaps a little ache. No, it was nothing. But it was them at home who wanted her to come. And maybe she could get some medicine that would help her through her chores.

She clasped her hands and looked at her offspring, at the way they lived here, smiled a little at them, though perhaps not quite as she used to. Mother sat beside her, serious, didn't take her eyes off her. They were like two sisters, so alike. The paleness and the thin hair did it, the features that had the same fragility and calm. So alike in figure too, tough and stocky. Mother briefly caressed the old hand, more she didn't want to show, it seemed, before the children. We must realize that Grandmother was old, she'd soon be seventy-eight, some things simply couldn't be the same as before. Well, they'd go off to the doctor's together, as soon as he opens, that's what they'd do. And so all would be well with Grandmother again. 'It's in God's hands,' said the old lady.

The children looked at the two of them, silent and

wondering – it was strange how serious Mother was. Furthest away stood Anders, white-faced and staring at Grandmother as if he wanted to see right through her. They didn't talk much more, the girls looked for something to tidy up in the kitchen, set out plates and porridge for the youngest two, who had to be off soon. Anders had to come to the table and eat, but he couldn't get anything down. Hurried to say goodbye and crept out through the door with a prolonged stare at the old lady.

He and his sister plunged forward through the snow in the direction of school. It was frosty and unnaturally quiet, the town was deserted, no footprints led from front doorsteps, as if no one lived in the houses. They strode one behind the other without saying anything.

Now the clock up in the tower rang out – Anders jumped, thought they were beginning to ring the church-bells! No, it was only the half-hour.

Children could be heard in the other streets, they came along in clusters, squealing and shoving. Down into the church park they came upon their slides under the snow, got up speed and shot away in a long line, tumbling and staggering up again. Anders and his sister kept behind, made little slides without actually taking runs, as if they didn't belong with the others today.

They had two hours to go before break. Anders sat trying to follow the words being read, trying to cling to them so as not to be alone, trying to be among the others. But he was hardly concentrating. While he listened tensely, heard exactly what was said, he *thought* how he was now sitting here listening – which meant of course that he wasn't really listening at all.

What were they talking about – the words just beat against the walls, bounced right across the room, and meant nothing.

And so they were talking about God – here too, here and at home, everywhere! Who was it? What did all that talk mean? Did they think it helped?

No, he didn't bother so much about God. Not like before. And he had never really understood him – not that that mattered.

Yet – if he could only run into the forest, if he could get an hour free and run out there as fast as possible, dash off before it was too late, run, run, so that he would get there quite worn out, panting and excited, and then collapse on the stone . . .

If he could get free, say that he *must*, that there was something more important than anything else, that he simply had to rush away . . . !

No, no one would understand. What would he say? That he had to run out into the forest! Who would understand that? That one must beg and pray on one's knees, positively aflame with zeal, on a stone . . . pray that they should live, that they should live . . . !

He was quite worked up, didn't know what was happening round about him. Didn't notice the pause between classes, how they'd come in again, got another teacher, something else was being talked about . . .

Yes – they talked about so much. It was as if they didn't realize it all came down to one single thing. They were always thinking about something else. Not about the fact that they would die, that they would die . . .

The bell went and they got out, scuffed and yelled in the corridor. In the playground they threw snowballs at each other's heads, the last battle before lunch.

Anders and his sister crept home silently: They didn't know whether to hurry or to take their time. Towards the end they were practically running.

But Grandmother still hadn't come back from the doctor's. Only children were at home, sitting waiting.

Anders clambered up to the window, sat watching, crouched, as if ready to leap. His heart was thumping, his eyes were hot as if he had a fever.

Then they came, Mother and Grandmother walking up the path calmly and quietly. They were both like old ladies, both in kerchiefs, but Mother had a cloak with ties. They greeted a railwayman, and a cook who was leaning out of the kitchen window, then vanished inside.

Came into the room to be greeted by all the children, sat down and made their report.

There was nothing to be done for Grandmother. No, it was too late. The doctor had examined her carefully and had been so kind and friendly. But nothing would help. It was cancer and it had gone too far. 'Well, well,' said the old lady. 'God's will be done.'

Mother did the talking, not her. The old lady only added a few words here and there. 'It was remarkable,' she said, 'how kind and good he was with me.' She had heard he could be hard on people, many hesitated to go to him. But with her he had sat and talked in a friendly way as if to a child. And he wouldn't take any payment, just said she didn't likely have much to spare. She thought that was very kind of him. He would be very expensive for he was highly qualified. Yes, a remarkable person.

The children stood round in a circle, sniffling. Behind and a little apart stood Anders, deathly pale, his rigid face forward, staring intently at the old lady. Mother and she were sitting there under the windows, which were iced over. They weren't taking the news as something dreadful. Well, Mother did have an air of being somehow transfigured, just as if she weren't actually present. But she kept on patting Grandmother on the hand and fussing a little with her, adjusting her kerchief, straightening the fold in her skirt. Something had been changed between the two of them – Grandmother was like a child taken in hand and tended by her prudent mother. She seemed bewildered by what had happened to her, at times taken up by it in an outward manner, as if it were an event. Sat stroking the kerchief that lay on her lap, the fine wedding kerchief with the pressed roses. Then she seemed to be thinking that the children were standing there wondering how long she would come to go on living among them. And she said that she had asked the doctor, for she wanted to know how it was, so that when her time came she would be prepared. But he had turned away and answered that he didn't know. Then she understood him well and regretted having asked. 'No,' I said to the doctor, 'that's something *we* know nothing about.'

The trains shunted to and fro outside, it was the start of the busiest period of the day in the marshalling yard. The smoke swept along the window panes so that the ice melted. Mother said they would now have a drop of coffee. Yes, that would be fine, said the old lady, and the girls were sent to get it ready.

So they sat and drank coffee, round the table, not

saying much. The children sighed, bent over their cups, now and then had to pull out a hankie, weep surreptitiously. Anders didn't want anything, he just walked to and fro, crept round among them, stepping on the mats, over to the windows and down to the door, his face white. His eyes were quite dry, as if lustreless. At one point the old lady met his rigid stare and nodded, smiled a little to him. But nothing in his face changed and he couldn't look her in the eye.

When they'd finished their coffee the old lady got up. 'Yes, time I went back home. You'll be coming out to see me, dear children.'

Then it broke out, the children couldn't keep their tears back. Mother too had tears in her eyes, but she wasn't crying. 'Of course, Mother,' she said, 'more than before.' 'It's nice you don't forget us,' said the old lady.

It was the first time death had come close to them there at home, which was why it seized them so strongly. They felt how completely they belonged together, couldn't grasp that any one of them should go away, should be missed, not exist among them any more. All the warmth they had within themselves broke out so that as never before they felt as one. And this helped and strengthened them in their grief.

Only Anders stood as if outside the warm stream that flowed through them. He crept halfway into the other room and watched them from there, not a tear in his eyes. The children were clustered round the old lady, clumsily patting her. But not him. It looked as if he didn't love her as much as the others did.

'I have one or two errands in town,' said the old lady while they helped her on with her shawl and fastened it behind her back. Some nuts from the ironmonger's for the chaff-cutter. A hecto of snuff from Lundgren's for Emil, he says he likes that kind better than others. Then they must have half a kilo of coffee for the slaughtering next week. Mother asked her to promise to keep away from the slaughtering, it could be so cold, she wouldn't be able to take it. 'You well know I'll have to be there,' she retorted. 'There's no mercy for me yet.'

Then at the door she said, 'I don't see how they'll manage when I'm gone, it's much too dear with paid folk from outside, it never works.'

She tied her kerchief and adjusted it on her head. 'Well, I'll be on my way. And thank you.'

So off she went, the milk-can in her hand.

Grandmother lived for another year. In the summer she managed to help with the haymaking, and then too with the rye-harvest, a little, but then she had to take to her bed. They went out to visit her often, between trains, to see how things were with her. Anders didn't want to go. He found this or that excuse and usually they let him stay at home. Yet now and then he had to go. As they approached the farm he would turn paler and paler. When they came in and he had to shake her by the hand it was as if he did so against his will. He almost didn't look at her, at least not in the eye. The others were as usual, didn't want to admit anything was wrong, only wanted to be as good as possible to her. For him she was already transformed, as if she were already dead. At times she gazed at him steadily. Perhaps she thought he wasn't as attached to her as she'd believed.

As soon as he could he crept out. Walked up and

down in the garden. The flowers had no scent, none of Grandmother's flowers, that were everywhere. He idled past the gooseberry bushes, remembered how he used to lie beneath them, in the glaring sun – and then she would come out and stand on the step. He looked into the arbour, where she used to sit shelling peas, it was just a big empty hole. Everything was changed, nothing as it used to be. And yet the sun still shone, as in the middle of the day, in the middle of summer. But everything here was now *marked.* It wasn't right.

He crawled through the hawthorn hedge and stood looking out over the countryside. It was quite empty. The fields lay there, stony properties separated by fences, and the farmsteads scattered widely – there, and there, and there. Yet it was quite empty. And over the marshlands it was as if a hand had passed, everything wiped out, nothing left. Everything here was *marked.* It *wasn't right.*

Someone came out and called him. He ducked behind the hedge.

Then he crept over to the outhouse, looked through the little window opening into the stall where she would move among the cows at milking time. It smelled warm and good and milky there, especially on winter evenings, coming in from the cold. She would lean her forehead against the cow she was milking and if anyone came in she'd hear nothing because of the frothing in the pail. He wandered behind the outhouse, into a patch of maple and juniper, skirted round it. Crept round the farmhouse – looked at the windows of the room where he knew she and all the others were sitting.

At last it was time for them to go and catch the

train. Then he came inside and said goodbye to her, with the others. She looked steadily at him again. It was as if she realized that he didn't care so much about her as the others did.

It always felt like that, it tormented him.

There was one time he remembered specially – he and Mother arrived one day that summer. As they came up the pathway they saw the old lady, she was pulling potatoes. Just a handful or so, for dinner. She was kneeling on the earth, because the pain prevented her from stooping. When she'd finished she couldn't get up again, he and Mother had to help her up. At first she had difficulty standing, as if she only wanted to sink down again, and her eyes were like glass, as if she weren't seeing them. He was trembling as if he too were going to collapse, unable to hold himself upright and unable to support her. But Mother brushed the earth off her and helped her in.

Then he had to get away from them, leant against the side of the house and wept. It was the only occasion he was able to weep.

In his fear of death there was something inhuman. He had, it seemed, no sympathy. Everything was swallowed by his fear of what was happening to her. He saw her constantly, before his eyes, every day, from morning to evening. But in a way he wasn't thinking about *her,* only about the fact that she was going to die. About the dreadful fact that right among them someone was walking around and dying. It was as if he didn't know who it was. When he did remember, he clung fast to the memory of how she had been before, when she was living, when she wasn't going to die. Now she no longer existed, one felt she wasn't here, that she didn't belong here. One had to *remember* her.

There was something inhuman in this frantic clinging to life – something inimical to life itself.

During winter, since she was bedridden, the old lady faded away slowly. She left them gradually, could no longer see them so clearly and couldn't always follow what they told her. She could no longer keep abreast with the jobs around the farm, sometimes she would ask, wanted to find out about this or that – but when they answered her it was as if she weren't listening. One evening she'd asked where she was lying. And when they told her she was in the little side room she was suprised, she'd thought the room was much bigger.

This, and similar news, was recounted on the note that came with the milk. Early each morning it arrived with a few lines from out there. It was a cold winter and the note was always frozen, Mother had to breathe on it so that it could be unfolded without the writing being obliterated. More and more frequently she went out there, and towards the end she stayed there. It was she and the old man, her father, who kept watch over the dying one. He sat by the window and read from the Bible. She tended the invalid, tiptoed silently in and out, bent down and listened to the whispered wants. The old man couldn't hear her any longer. But she whispered to Mother that she could hear when he read. So he sat there, reading aloud. The snow lay in drifts high up against the windows, in other parts the earth was bare and many fruit trees were killed by the frost that winter.

All the children were out there one evening to say goodbye to her, but by then she could hardly distinguish between them. A few days later Mother wrote, with the milk, that the end had come.

To Anders it was almost a relief. The children went round talking about Grandmother all day, about how she was *then* and *then* – often from long ago – about what she said *that* time, about how *early* she always got up in the mornings, about the figure-of-eight biscuits she could bake, about how she looked after her flowerbed, her peonies, about how once when she was a girl she got lost in the forest and had to turn her cardigan back-to-front to bring her luck back – about everything. Anders took part eagerly, all the time. He also remembered – yes, much! He talked, he remembered – and wherever it was they were talking, in the kitchen, in the room, he was there. He was flushed with enthusiasm and his eyes shone. . . It was as if she were alive again!

Mother came home to sew, to prepare for the funeral. The girls, and both boys, all had something to do. Anders was being confirmed that year so he got his black clothes earlier than his classmates. He'd never had black before. It felt strange. People looked at one, at the mourning crêpe round one's cap. Especially when they all went together, Mother as well perhaps, all in black – people looked at them and stepped aside, greeted them in a special way. It became oppressive, walking through the street together. It felt as if one were not like the others.

On Sunday morning they set out for the funeral, early. Twigs had been spread on the snow before the gate and all the way up to the door. The garden looked cold in the raw weather, but inside it was warm. Some had already arrived, mostly old people who were warming their fingers at the open hearth where the spruce logs were burning and crackling, spitting out sparks into the floor. Everything had been scrubbed and the old ladies stepped only on the mats, whispering and exchanging greetings, a handkerchief crumpled in one hand. When the mourners from town arrived, Mother and Father and all the grand-children, an even greater silence fell. All the old ones came forward and shook hands, holding on for a long time. Little or nothing was said. In the middle of the floor stood a tall fellow with a red beard, who had moved into the district only a few years ago, he was talking loudly.

More and more arrived. Conveyances stopped down by the outhouse and old ladies wrapped in shawls stepped out. All the time people were coming up the garden, for the most only old people. Others could be seen plodding along the roads, coming this way too, those who had no means of transport. Many of these had been invited, here on the farm they didn't have a horse either but they'd borrowed one for the funeral. One after another they stepped in, tall, thin farm women, toothless and with sagging breasts, in black dresses that smelled of naphtha, and men from neighbouring farms in big baggy clothes. The whole house filled, in the rooms above, where the onions and the apples had been removed from the floor, there were more people, their steps could be heard below.

Then the door into the side-room downstairs was opened and an icy draught passed through the whole house. They solemnly crowded in. The smell of scrubbing rose from the floor which hadn't been able to dry in the cold, the scattered twigs of spruce smelled wet from the snow still in them, it had hardly melted. Everyone crowded forward to see her for the last time, to say farewell. Old ladies who had always known her, whose heads shook with age, young farm wives who couldn't remember her different from how she lay now, old and grey, old men who danced with her at Harakulla when they were young, farm lads from Bolsgård and Jutagårn who'd had coffee and a dram with Emil. Anders didn't push forward. He looked between those who stood closer, saw a little of the forehead and some thin hair; when someone moved aside, and he saw the mouth gaping, the jaw having fallen slightly, then he shivered and wedged himself in behind the others so that he could see nothing. But Helge, his elder brother, stood forward by her all the time. Of all the children it was he who had loved her most, had been most with her, and in a way it didn't frighten him that she was dead, it didn't astonish him. He had helped her to fork and turn hay, had weeded turnips and mown vetches, caught perch and roach for her in the river, emptied traps in the mornings and come home with eels almost before she was up. In a sense he belonged more out here than he did in town, and no one looked more like the family out here than he did. He stood weeping silently and stilly, because he had loved her.

When they began to put the lid on, Anders felt he wanted to rush forward. They had to wait a little because Grandfather wanted to stroke her cheek first. It seemed to take ages too before they had the lid firmly screwed down. But when it was done he felt how terrible it was that he, alone of them all, hadn't properly said goodbye to her. And now it was too late, he calmed down, noticed how he too could begin to cry, like the others.

Jacob, a venerable old man with snow-white hair

flowing down over his shoulders, started a psalm. His voice was cracked but didn't waver, he'd been churchwarden for most of his life and had sung for such occasions as long as he could remember. Then the coffin was carried out.

The horses stood restively stamping before all the sledges, wanted to be on the move. The men in their top-hats growled at them, held them by the bridles till the coffin was placed. It lay on the first sledge and the farm boy from Jutagårn drove it because it was their horse. In the outhouse the cows mooed, the hens pecked at the oats beneath the shafts. Now everyone was ready and they set off.

At the gate stood Grandfather, too poorly to accompany them, and waved for as long as they could be seen on their way. 'I'm coming soon Stina,' was the last he had said.

The road to the church followed the river, whose edges were frozen. And the marshes were frozen, the whole countryside. The farmsteads looked so bare, as they do in winter when the trees don't give the covering we are used to seeing. They stood as if deserted. Nearly everyone was of course at the funeral, sitting there in the long line of sledges that looked like a wagon-train, so heavily loaded that it could scarcely drag itself forward. The runners scraped where the earth was bare and the travellers sat shaking on their seats and looking about them. At the front on the coffin sat the farm boy among a few flowers from town.

When they could be seen from the church the ringing began. The flaps in the bell-tower stood open and the bells rang out over the whole neighbourhood, the wastelands and the scattered hamlets, right up to farmsteads away in the forest. And as far as it was heard the men took off their hats, as the custom was, and the women curtseyed. In a hamlet up at the very edge of the parish a little old lady sat by a window, wrapped in a shawl so that she could have the window open. She was the oldest in the congregation, shrunk and stooped, hadn't left her cottage for many years, but her hair was coal-black, without one grey strand, her eyes sparkled brown. She was Father's mother. Perhaps she had some Walloon blood, perhaps not – there was something foreign about her for she was dark in a way no one else around here was. And she seemed in a manner finer than the farm wives, although she was poorer than they were; as a girl she'd been allowed some schooling along with the daughters of the gentry. But now she was sitting there listening with her Bible on her knee and the window open to the bells being rung for old mother Stina, and when the first tolls reached her she clasped her hands and leaned out with her strange little head, so that the sparrows on the sheaf tied to the window-sill scattered into space.

The church stood on a hillock insignificant as all the other hillocks in that part of the country. They stopped down below and carried the coffin up the slope. The bells clanged right above their heads; out among the graves stood pale girls from the confirmation class, holding each other by the hand and looking uneasily at the procession, it was the time of year when confirmations were approaching both in town and out here.

The burial service took place in the church. Anders knew that now it would start – the hardest bit. When the organ pealed out, it was for them to begin singing the most horrible psalm, the most unpleasant words he knew. He pressed himself into the pew and stared straight ahead. But they joined in the psalm as if ecstatically, clear children's voices from the gallery and the whole congregation, all the old ones down here, the din of the organ breaking under the arches:

I walk to Death each step I tread . . .

It was as if no kind of life existed, as if it didn't need to exist – what use would it be? They seemed stupefied, as if they gave themselves to something close and precious, more certain than anything else. And the priest was reading: Of earth. . .

If only it would come to an end, if only it would stop! This long ceremony around death – it was terrible.

And then, out to the grave!

Everyone in the church came, those uninvited coming last. The newly opened tomb could be seen at some distance because the lumps of earth lay in a huge pile beside it, they'd had to pry and prod their way down through the ground-frost, which was three feet thick. Everyone gathered round and there could be heard the noise of her being lowered.

This however wasn't as hard as he'd thought it would be. Everything that happens outside is easier. The cold wind was chilling. And snow got into galoshes. Boys he played with stood looking at him. It wasn't so shut in and solemn. When he tossed his flowers into the grave he managed to cry.

Then they all went in to take part in communion.

Afterwards they journeyed home, the whole long line of them. A little snow had scurried down so the sledges ran more easily, over the bare patches too. The horses were allowed to go as they pleased so it didn't take long. Grandfather stood on the front step and received everyone, gazed at the empty sledge that came last. Mother recounted everything for him, how it went, the whole funeral from beginning to end. He asked too about the surface of the snow, how it was for the sledges, something she'd forgotten to tell him about.

But dinner was waiting, set on two long tables forming a right angle, there was a great deal of food and when the kitchen door swung open steam billowed in. The old ladies would glance sidelong at the table, the men rubbed their cold hands and waited for a dram.

They sat down and remained sitting until evening. Dishes were handed round, the one after the other, simple, but many of them and much of each. One had to take something from every one, at least once, though some of them were almost alike. It was a superfluity that nourished, not just tasted good. The men drank spirits with their food. For the first hour they were solemn. But gradually they became talkative and spoke right across the table and from one end to the other, holding forth. They sat so closely packed they could scarcely move. The chairs which had been borrowed from here and there were jammed together and down by the door there was only a plank to sit on and the bench that stood in the arbour in summer-time. When one of the men by the wall wanted out all the others had to shift themselves, it could hardly be managed discreetly, and the women who never got out complained good-naturedly. The longer the meal lasted the livelier it became and the warmth in the room filled everyone. In the open hearth the log-fire seemed to be thriving in the heat. They began to sweat.

The sense of well-being increased. They talked and talked. Old fellows with a bit of a reputation for being comics livened up and began to feel their way with a broad grin, began vying with each other. Those nearby listened, the women with their heads aslant. Other men sat talking seriously, about cows that were about to calve, chalk and superphosphate, covered drains and the cultivation of moss. But with raised voices, so that everyone would hear what they thought about matters, their current opinions.

Apart from farmers there was Massa-Janne, a diminutive tailor, born and bred in the parish. He spat when he talked and had sewn all the clothes of the big fellows here. When he took measurements he had to stand on a stool, irritable because the stool was unavoidable, but spitting on his customers all the time in compensation. And the miller, the only really fat man at the funeral, with a backside that bulged over the chair seat and between the bars of the back. Anders, who was sitting next to him, saw that the tuft of hair in his ear was floury. And crouched on the garden bench right down by the door sat Peter Pot-luck, a thin fellow who also didn't have any land. He never said anything and he never looked up, only sat stooped with his tousled head over his plate. It was said that he ate nothing for several days if he thought he was going to be invited somewhere. Sometimes he was wrong and simply had to start eating again. At home he had boiled potatoes and old bread in his bread-bin, which he hurriedly shut if someone came. But the truth more likely was that he was poor and needed food, both his own and others'. And that was something no one mentioned, though there was a bit of teasing now and then. He sat right down by the door because he was the least special of all and because it was more shadowy there, so it wouldn't be noticed how much he put away.

About five o'clock, after the meat dishes, the desserts started; darkness had already fallen. All the food which the guests had brought was now to be set out, cheese-cakes, sweet-cheeses, many of each kind. They were more or less alike, but one recognized one's own on the tablecloth round the copper dish and each wife saw to it that everyone tasted hers. Nothing is quite so satisfying. They sat up and breathed deeply out of sheer enjoyment, which they all felt they deserved, even Peter came out of his obscurity a little and stared silently a little of the way up the table.

Anders thought it was fine with all this hubbub and warmth, all the old ladies and men talking and eating and not being as they had been earlier. It felt so secure in here. The fire crackled and the heat gave a feeling of sleepiness. He sat at the wall. Behind their backs the window panes were inky black, but inside there was no lack of light. In the middle of the long table stood the big paraffin lamp and out at the end the little one, down by the door candles, the whole room was lit up. But in the place of honour beside the priest sat Mother, pale and quiet, in a sense pale because of all the light. Wasn't she talking to anyone?

Dinner was nearly over. The last and finest dish was a cake from town, decorated in black and white, with a big black cross in the middle. It was much admired, everyone had to taste it. Anders shivered when it approached him. He let it go past, although he could imagine he had never tasted anything so good. The miller took a big piece of the cross and swallowed it at one go.

So at last they rose, the priest solemnly said grace.

Doors were opened and people spread out. The porch was full of clothes as if an entire parish lived in the house, it was hardly possible to squeeze through between the piles of outer clothes that smelled of hay and the byre. But in the rooms upstairs it was empty, and quite cool after the warmth downstairs. A faint scent lingered from the apples and the onions, behind the mirror was a sprig of lavender grandmother used to take a little of when she went to church. Coffee was served up here. With cakes for the ladies and brandy for the men. Soon it was warm and full of people here too, they talked and enjoyed themselves

Anders didn't quite know where to take himself. He was the youngest, had no one of his own age to be with. He drifted around a little, here or there, or stood by a wall now and then. Nudged open the kitchen door, as was his habit; only strangers there, washing up and sorting things out, and huge piles of china that didn't belong here, the plates had a rose in the middle. And so he wandered upstairs, looked into the rooms, sat down and listened. In the one room sat the women, while in the other the men were booming over their toddy glasses, it was full of smoke and everyone was talking at once, no one listening to anyone, sheer noise and high spirits. He felt happier there. Nonetheless he went back down after a while. On the pasteboard of the stairway wall there was an artless painting showing the road from the farm to the church, the farm at the bottom and the church at the top with a few crosses and birches round it, and the road itself winding along the bannister. But today he didn't look at it, hurried down, past it. Opened the outside door, stepped out.

It was utterly dark. Cold but totally still, no wind. A few men stood among the gooseberry bushes, peeing, they were big and broad in the darkness, it splashed out like from horses. To the east the sky was clear, with a few stars, otherwise clouded over. When the men went in he was left there standing alone in the quietness.

A light shone down in the outhouse, he could see it, in the little window that looked in to the cows, but it wasn't very distinct, the window was covered with spiders' webs. Soon someone came out of the outhouse with the milk pail in one hand and the lantern in the other. She came up the path. The glimmer fell on the grey skirt that reached to her feet and it travelled along the path before her. When she came near the lit-up house she turned off and took the path round to the kitchen. He saw she was a middle-aged woman he didn't know.

Down by the river the ice was creaking, freezing over, he realized it was cold and that he was here only to do what the men had been doing. But he went over to the apple-tree by the side wall, that was where he had always gone.

Noise and voices came from the whole house. It was so packed with people one would expect it to collapse, talkative people, a people who are not talkative often. He stood there with his back to the house. Then through the confusion of voices there penetrated a voice that didn't seem to be speaking to anyone, a calm and clear voice that nothing disturbed, that no one answered.

He turned round. Low on the side wall there was a window that seemed strangely quiet, as if there were no one inside. It belonged to the little side room – he stood watching it.

When he was finished he walked over to it and looked in. There sat Grandfather upright in the bed where his old wife had died, he was reading out of the Bible that lay on the sheepskin before him. He had a clean shirt, quite new, one could see, the linen unbleached. And the sheets had never been used, they were completely smooth. His newly combed hair fell down over his shoulders, each strand lay straight. He sat solemnly, as if at a ceremony. The spruce twigs still lay on the floor, in the corner tall juniper bushes.

Anders was breathing on the window so it became misty. He wanted to go but he wiped the glass and lingered on. The crust of the snowdrift against the wall here wouldn't hold him any longer, he sank through. He could feel the twigs on the flowerbed beneath the snow. He had to pull himself up as far as he could in order to see, the lower part of the pane was iced over.

The old man was sitting motionless. Upstairs they were chattering and shrieking, he didn't notice, perhaps didn't hear. Read in the loud voice he had always used, the toothless mouth moved. Anders could hear each word.

At last he closed the Bible and clasped his hands over it. 'Amen. In the name of God Almighty. Amen.' But when he had set the Bible on the chair beside the bed he looked into the room and spoke again. 'The Lord thy God shall awake thee on the last day.' Then he lay down and blew the light out, and the darkness seemed just to swallow him.

Anders was now a youth. He began to wander around town and far out on the country roads with or without friends, as if he no longer felt at ease at home. He felt such a strange pressure there now. There was something oppressive and heavy in all that confinement at home. In the way everything belonged together, the people and the things they had around them, it was all so much of a piece. The old furniture, and the air in the rooms, the rag mats, woven out at the grandparents' place, and the people who walked about on them – there was a sameness binding it all together. When one came through the door and greeted those who happened to be inside – it was simply a matter of coming home. And when they sat round the lamp after supper and the sisters worked away at their crochet and the lamp-light reached halfway up the wall and the trains could be heard outside – then it was just an evening here at home. Father and Mother read the Bible, as they always did, serious and oppressed by the words. It felt like a weight on one's chest. And yet everything was tranquil. All security and peace. Why was it like this!

Everyone belonged together. They had everything in common. Sat as if enclosed in a special room, separated from the world. Lived one and the same life, and it seemed unchanging.

It was only a family, not special people – one had to break out, become a separate person!

And now he was beginning to break out.

It wasn't noticed. No one could notice it. Nothing

about them could be easily shown, given outward expression. Things simply dug themselves in, hid themselves, one could scarcely understand what was happening oneself. They only felt. They only felt everything. And now this was what he was feeling. Groping through it, crouching, as if in a cellar.

There was something raw about what was happening, like a birth. And birth-like anguish and throes, anxiety for a new awaking life and for an old one. And something sickening – because something was dissolving, changing, almost going rotten. What was changing! Why was it changing!

Animals drag themselves away when they are going to give birth, into their hole, into the darkness, where no one can hear their cries and where they bite through the cord, whimpering. And the blind offspring sniffs at the blood being sucked in by the earth . . .

Belonging to a family – why!

He was tormented by what was going on inside him. Carefully felt each small transformation, to be certain of keeping up, all the time. Almost enjoying it . . .

For the first time he realized how disconnected and dishonest life is. How incompletely and falsely one can live, things still go on. Life forces one into this and contrives that one gets along. Everything slides away from beneath – still, things go on. For the first time he was not living in the middle of himself. So far that was what he had always done.

It was the beginning of youth, the most dreadful of the ages of man. Rightly so, for it is the falsest, the most unreliable, the most inferior. Those who never discovered this have been false to the point of self-deceit. Childhood, adulthood, old-age, these can all be meaningful and genuine for us. Youth is something unworthy of a real human. The rootlessness of a personality, irresponsible freedom, a frightening dissolution, insecurity, dishonesty to life itself – but unworthy of a human. It's not suprising that empty phrase-mongers write about it, for that's where they flourished. It was their time. A time when most was offered and least demanded. – But he still found himself only at the beginning.

He crept away from their God, sneaked off without it being noticed. Soon he was standing out in the darkness and round about him there was only empty space. He shivered, as if he felt voluptuous. He felt how it *is* – only empty. That the emptiness was there, *he* well knew. He'd known that for long enough, as long as he could remember. In that case it was better to feel it properly, to stand out in the middle of the darkness. And so it was easier. A large destiny to bear.

If he could only stand still there in the darkness, only exist there. That would be no fate to complain about, it would suit him well. In the darkness – he could thrive there.

But he was going to die. Soon. Everyone knew. Didn't they? He was going to die of the chest complaint he had just got. People always kept a few steps away from him so that he couldn't pass the disease on to them. His brothers and sisters too, though they hid it a little more, didn't want him to notice too obviously. That cut him to the heart even more. They could have saved themselves. He would have liked to scream in their faces.

That they always kept about two steps away from him wasn't so easy to see. Could there be any doubt about it! Didn't he have eyes! He didn't perhaps notice everything, each expression, each tone, each little word, including those whispered in the kitchen, in the little room, where they shut themselves in – they would close the door between the rooms, it had never been closed before! Couldn't he feel that they had already begun to grieve for him . . . Couldn't he feel their oppression, an oppressive anguish in the house – the terrible fact that someone was walking about among them and dying! He saw everything, he understood everything. That was *easy*.

Only Mother showed nothing, no matter how close she came. But then she was above and beyond both sickness and death, beyond everything, couldn't be counted as belonging here. She was so good. Afraid lest he should notice the slightest hint, everything was to be as usual, he wasn't to suspect a thing, only feel how loved he was, especially now, how they thought about him – he and his sickness were never out of her mind, she wanted to be near him constantly, as one couldn't be certain how long . . . She gave herself away more than any of the others did!

Now in the spring he got an egg each lunchtime when he came in from school, something the others didn't get, she said he needed it. Each lunchtime it was there waiting for him like a reminder . . . in case he had forgotten. And she would sit down on the chair next to his and talk – there were plenty of other chairs round the kitchen table, only he and mother were at home during the break, she didn't have to sit just there! Talked about everything except what they were both thinking about, talked as if to distract him in his febrility, and so mildly it cut him to the quick, never a reproach, never a hard word, though he had stopped saying grace at meals, she forgave everything, made nothing of it. – He couldn't tolerate her tenderness. If he could only hate her!

All this goodness and lovingness at home – one couldn't put up with it. Never a raw blast swept in here. They sat in there, enclosed, protected, cosy, in a peace which bound them together but which didn't liberate them, didn't help them. Within them was a warmth that never caught fire but merely went on warming them, none of it was wasted, no flame could be seen. . . That was doubtless why it made one feel so anxious and oppressed, for it was never allowed to break out into flame, it never burned up. It was something they kept only for warming themselves. And this fear of God which his parents had was so heavy and aged, an ancient peace they sought to feel – through sighs, only sighs. It weighed one down and down – it seemed to want to suffocate. – One must break out!

No, the new doctrine one adopted, that swept God and all hope quite away, that exposed life open and raw, in all its nakedness, all its methodical lack of meaning – that helped better, that was more like it. And of course it was true. It wasn't just a belief – it reflected things as they are.

Since he was about to die, nothing much mattered. But he had to break out anyway! Out there, where it was rawer, colder – one could breathe for the short time left.

It was good to know it was empty there. It made one ready for what was coming. Perhaps one could get used to emptiness, and so no longer think of it as something terrible, no longer need to live so feverishly and anxiously for the short time . . .

No, he could never get used to it. Yet he sucked up the doctrine, greedily, gorged on it. It seemed to be made for him. It helped him, made his heart harder. And it accounted for much in his childhood, all the desolation and anguish waiting in ambush in the surrounding gloom, despite the security of home, despite all he had there . . . He'd been right! Now he was even more right, even more.

He became neither calm nor happy from all this, but that's as may be. All was on the move, no firm ground, and he moved with it. Nothing was certain, nothing stood fast – one could soon believe whatever one liked. Only the emptiness was forever unchanging, all around. Only anguish gnawed and gnawed, ate its hole within one – in one's breast, it felt, the hole grew and grew . . .

When he was tired, when he thought how he was only going to die anyway, he would think he might as well give up – what was the use of tearing oneself loose. Rather sink to rest in the safe embrace of home, where everything was so sure, and Mother would sit and hold his hand and read to him out of the psalm book, as she certainly would, as he knew she certainly would . . .

No, that wouldn't do. Things must be as they *were*. Even if one is about to die, one must live life as it is – here at home the security and peace were smothering! One must break out!

That he understood. He persisted.

Felt hot . . . Was often so hot all over, as if burning . . . Caused of course by his illness, the fever . . . Or by forces that were wakening, which had lain hidden in the child and were now erupting, deaf and unconscious, more and more stifling . . . Perhaps it was those which made him glow. He didn't know. No one knew. One drifted away, no one knew where to . . . And only this tentative rawness as a helpless defence, an attempt to understand what it was about and to cover over all his uncertainty and his longing both for others and for himself.

But he was going to die. Nothing mattered, he was only going to die. Just waited – nothing more. He stood outside, in a way. Like someone standing listening at a door.

That was how he felt. That, approximately, was where he had reached.

But life is mercifully jumbled and inconsistent. Not least for him, who was perpetually leaping from one thing to the next.

In reality he was mostly happy and cheerful. No one could notice anything different, often not even himself.

The smallest things could make him skip with pleasure. Simply because it was sunny for a while. Or because a shower of rain came after a sunny spell. Or because of nothing at all, simply because things stayed as they were. Because of anything. If only he came up out of his cellar the world lay wonderfully open for him. Nothing wrong with it, clear visibility all round. And what was good and orderly in it was then quite tangible. If he wished, all he needed to do was stick his head out of the little window . . .

What he was living through inside himself was mixed with many other experiences, something of everything. In winter for instance, when they went skating, for most of the day usually, they'd go off out over the lakes which lay everywhere. Where one lake ended the second began. They'd clamber on their points over the isthmus, set off on the next lake. When school was closed for cleaning they could start early in the morning frost and with the groaning of the ice, men stood ice-fishing away out there, small as dots. If one skated right up to them they would scarcely open their lips, merely glare. As if unconcerned, one did a quiet 'American' and shot off again. It was possible to go as far as the linesman's place at Näset, turn round the point and scare the hens with wild turns, so that they scrambled madly up towards the house. Here as in many places there were currents, for a river entered the lake, they had to be watched, sometimes there were tussocks, sometimes not. Islets large and small one could skate round. And on the shore to the north-east were the bathing places, which looked strange now in winter, hard to recognize the bush where one undressed.

Late in the evening they collected reeds and made a bonfire, came whirling in from the little inlets with big armfuls, straight on to the fire, tossing them in mid-swing. The flames leapt high, flakes poured here and there in the draught. The ice melted, creaked with the warmth and because too many of them were standing around. It cracked. Rumbled far out in the darkness.

Red and famished they arrived home, dried their skates by the open fire. Suffered from ingrown toenails and were given warmed-up food, both dinner and supper had long since passed.

It was a great life. Nothing wrong with it. It was different from his. And yet wasn't he really part of it too?

Indeed he lived different kinds of life, two at least. And he felt they had nothing to do with each other.

No matter how exhilarated, he could cut himself right off. But the joyful freshness could also be cut right off.

However, he thrived living like this, in different ways. It was exciting. Much need too, when one had such a short time . . .

That illness, what was it really? When he wasn't thinking about it he felt not the slightest pain. One should be a little careless, let it go as it wished. It did so anyway.

He had friends, went about with them. One was called Jonas, a fine boy, from the country, he was studying for something. In the winter they'd have many deep discussions, in the summer they'd catch pike. Jonas had a wooden arm, as a child he'd lost his right arm in a threshing machine. But he was more dexterous than anyone, could do everything with his left hand and much better than others. He was especially adept at catching pike, their summer pastime, when Anders lived out at his place, several miles from town. There were lakes there too, several of them. One with low miry grass-covered banks was particularly good, they could crawl right out to the edge where the pike lay dozing in the hot sunlight. Shoes had already been left behind, up at the edge of the wood far from the lake, moving silently was still not easy and became more and more difficult in the wet mud. Jonas always kept in front, which was only right, he was the one who could take them. Anders clambered after, was liable to be scolded. If he squelched too much Jonas threatened him with his single arm and a deathly silence fell all around. He was impossible. Crouching and squatting along the edge, he saw the pike at a great distance, far ahead, where they drowsed beneath the lily-pads. He'd somehow wangle the loop of gut over the fish's head and that would be that. It wasn't long before they had a whole stick full. He had to keep half an eye on envious people, both on shore and on some skiff protruding from the reeds. He was a terror to those who considered they owned the fish, those who couldn't catch any.

So there wasn't much boasting about how many they brought home. Jonas could well give them away on the road back. Sometimes there wasn't a fin left and his mother would mutter when they clattered into the cottage, crestfallen, then she'd produce coffee and buns.

The village where they stayed was peculiarly desolate, at least Anders thought so, but that was perhaps because he was a stranger here. All the houses were unpainted and not too well cared for, often they didn't have curtains at more than three or four of the windows. Nothing much was cultivated either, no gardens, only naked ground, with a well and perhaps an apple-tree. Maybe it was because of that, but the spaces between the farms looked strangely empty and unfriendly, although the buildings were quite close together. It seemed as if people never visited each other, didn't even know each other properly. But Jonas knew everyone there, greeted them cheerfully – girls winding up water, farm lads with cart loads of manure or hay. And they were clearly accustomed to shaking hands with him, which at first looked rather awkward because he shook with his left hand.

There was a lot of forest around the village. And Jonas hunted too. He was notorious indeed. In one move he would swing up his shotgun and take aim otherwise he couldn't hold it steady. Shot hares and duck, woodcock, a bit of everything. And in the autumn woodgrouse, with a flare, which was illegal and in that part of the countryside quite unusual. He was handy at everything.They enjoyed themselves in the country. In the wintertime, in the town, it was different. They made themselves more presentable, their conversations became in every way more serious and enlightened as they strolled in the better part of town. But they would forget themselves now and then, roll about as if on a country lane. By nature Jonas had a strangely relaxed gait. As if nothing mattered too much. He had a habit of occasionally grasping his wooden arm, up at the shoulder, as if to make sure it was there. As he did so he would light up with a good-natured grin.

And he was a trifle vain too here in town. He insisted on wearing a glove on his artificial hand, as soon as one glove was worn and the wood showed through he would buy a new one. One fine spring, when he started going with a girl, he acquired a pale grey glove and was finer than ever. And a touch superior too. He had a little cunning smile that could have taken him far if he'd bothered. But he had already seen through the world, discovered how it was, more or less, and took himself back to his native parish, he may as well live there.

Then there was another friend, a small gnome-like fellow called Murre. They'd known each other from schooldays, then Murre had left and become a cycle-repairer. They met now only on Sundays when he was free. If they ran into each other on the street on a working day his fingers were greasy so he'd shake hands with no more than a thumb. But each Sunday he came with a high stiff double collar like a gentleman and they went out walking together, puffing cheap cigars which Murre was able to save up for both of them.

They usually took the line out to the forest and walked on the roads there. They had played there as boys, knew every inch. They talked of that time as of something far in the past, laughed indulgently when they noticed they could recall something or other. But if they happened to walk past the stone Anders had out there, he would look in the other direction and keep up a flow of eager talk. The stone was not something they had in common. Murre knew nothing about it.

Other friends too. One who never said a sensible word, who chose to be wise in that way. One who lived in beauty, none of the others knew what that was. And their discussions were all painstaking and prudent.

But there was much one could never talk with anyone about. Everything one really went around thinking of. Or simply bore with one, that weighed one down.

Having parted company with his Sunday friend, the cycle-repairer, towards evening, he often went back out to the stone. He was tired by then and in other ways too had little pleasure in going. Still, he went.

On the way he would try to think back to what it was like when they came here not so long before, he tried to imagine it was now more or less the same. Dusk had not yet fallen, it was still almost as light as it had been earlier. He thought too of many other things that occupied him, from day to day, and which gave him much pleasure, and of how he clung to all that, properly belonged to it! Didn't he have more joy out of everything than most of the others had? He could feel so filled with it, sometimes at least, with everything around him, with joy that came from . . . he didn't know where.

As he lived, walking about in the world, and looked around him, like now, this evening, out here on the line, wasn't he really and properly happy? As happy as the others. He was. Just like the others.

Whatever it was he had to drag along, privately, was just something he imagined. It meant nothing.

Like this compulsion to come out here. It had nothing to do with him, with anything that was him. Not now. As a child he had been driven by an inner need, had lain here in deep and fervent faith, as in an ecstasy. Then he had continued as if for the sake of going through the steps. At last it had become an empty convention.

No it wasn't even that. Signified nothing. Just a matter of walking out here.

And now he was standing there. Set himself on the same spot as always, the marks were visible in the grass. He didn't fall on his knees, hadn't done so for years. But he did clasp his hands, as hard as he could, so hard he could feel it in his whole body, really feel that he was clasping his hands. Which induced a certain numbness. And so he prayed.

But only that he should live. Nothing else. Only the same as before, as always. Only to live – nothing further about anything. Other things could be as they wished. Only that he wouldn't die.

He didn't think about any God. Had no belief. And not a single thought that this would help him in any way, give him inner strength, have some significance. It meant nothing.

What he prayed for didn't matter either. But there had to be something. And so it was always this, always the same thing.

No, it meant nothing. It was only a compulsion which he realized came from being overstrung.

He was free. He had broken out.

One autumn evening Anders was on his way through the town. He was going towards the northern part of town, almost out at the edge. It was cloudy and dull, a little while ago it had been raining. The streets were wet, they shone where there was a lamp post, only every second one was lit. It was empty, no one out, only a policeman at the corner by the square. There were lights in the windows there, but the blinds were down, sounds of a piano came from one of the houses. He continued, walking quickly, his collar turned up.

On North Street he turned in through a gateway, into a courtyard. It was almost pitch dark, hard to see, a few carts and piles of old junk, discarded wheels and rusty iron sheets stacked on each other. Far in was a little low house, lights burned, but the windows didn't give on to this side. Singing could be heard from inside, but faintly, as if the walls were very thick. But he could find his way, following the song, over to the entrance. Opened the door and stepped in.

It was a whitewashed room in semi-darkness, small windows, the ceiling like an arch. In the middle a rough pillar which was clearly there not to support but to conceal, so that the whole room could not be seen at once. Here were old ladies sitting crouched on unpainted benches, a few young men with their caps on their knees, young women too and, behind the pillar, some half-grown boys. At the front, a dais, where two paraffin lamps hung from the roof. And there in the light sat some soldiers of the Salvation Army, along the wall; forward, by the railing, two women officers were singing to a guitar. He sat down on a bench.

There was a fire on but it wasn't warm. Everyone had their outer clothes on. They sat in clusters, crowded together at the back of the hall where it was most shadowy, the front benches were empty. Down by the door sat mad Johan from the poorhouse, alone, his head thrust forward and his eyes gleaming in the dark. The walls dripped with dampness, where the plaster had come away they were sooty. It was an old disused smithy, rented out for this. The forge had stood in the middle, was walled in.

They sang – clearly and a little shrilly, but fervently, mostly the women. The guitars jingled. The song sounded shut in, as if in a cellar. The voices of the two officers rang out above the others, cleaner and more practised. They stood in the light, faces upwards, eyes burning, as in an ecstasy, never looked down at the book as the others did, knew it by heart. They were wearing their cloaks, buttoned up to the neck. One of them was dark and full-blooded, with something restrained discernible in her shining gaze and over her mouth when she opened her broad warm lips. The other was frail, almost like a child. The slender figure didn't seem to have any strength of its own but stood there in the light, abandoned to it. There was something touching about her, at the same time helpless and candid. Her face was pale, the features poorly, like those of a farm girl, not perhaps very fine but with a tenderness that made them much more beautiful. Her eyes weren't radiant, they just shone quietly, inwardly. Her hair fell forward from under the uniform hat, pale and fragile round her cheeks. She was in a way without colour. And yet burned like fire. Like a flame nourished by wax.

Anders sat and watched her all the time. He knew her.

They were working themselves up. Sang more eagerly, as if trying to make the glow within flame up. At first it seemed an effort of will. Then it broke out by itself, they were carried away, as if drugged. One of them began to witness. And the others joined in with mumblings. Thank you dear Jesus. Praise be to Thee. Hallelujah! Thanksgiving and praise. They sighed and prayed with their faces in their hands. One woman sat rocking to and fro. The soldier who was giving his testimony was egged on by them, spoke more vehemently, stood with his eyes shut, the words just poured out of his mouth. He was in a sort of trance. And the others were sucked along, it was like a wave that lifted them, heaved up and sank, drawing them all along. Someone further back started moaning. Furthest off, in the darkness, mad Johan sat staring with glazed eyes.

Anders felt more and more uneasy. It almost made him sick. And it was stuffy, scarcely possible to breathe.

They raved on. God wasn't named once, they spoke only of Jesus and again Jesus, which was something he found particularly repulsive, this was part of the faith which repelled him first, which became most alien to him. They sighed and exulted over nothing else. The very air hung heavy, it settled on one's breast, one gasped, couldn't inhale . . . It was something whipped up, over-heated – nothing for him.

Now it was her turn to witness, the young officer of salvation whom he knew. She took up her position by the railing and began talking without looking up. It was noticeable that she was unsure, not really accustomed to being an officer yet. But she shone. She told them how she'd been saved, how Jesus had come to her – Praise be! Glory and Honour! How he had raised her out of her sin and want and given her a new life. Now she felt so much better. Now she felt no unease over anything, as the children of the world do. All troubles she laid upon him. She said it so simply there was no mystery left. And yet there was a radiance streaming around her.

Anders sat in devotion, unmoving, never took his eyes from her. The boys were giggling behind the pillar. He shuddered as if he had wakened up. But forced himself not to hear, to notice nothing but her.

She became a little more fearless. Sometimes she raised her glance, looked out into the hall. But the murmuring of the prayers round about her didn't excite her, when they sighed and groaned she merely spoke in a slightly warmer voice. There was something so clean and poor about her where she stood in her cape of blue serge. It was worn. In some places it was quite shiny, mainly on the left side, where she was in the habit of carrying the bundle of papers when she was out selling the *Battle Cry*. But the worn parts were beautiful here in the lamplight. A kind of glow on the cloth. It suited her. At least Anders thought so. He never stopped looking at her, her face, which as she spoke became more naked, as if one were only now seeing her. The pale mouth appeared to smile when she opened it. But it was not a smile, just something pliant and good in the lips themselves. They were just like that.

When she had finished they began praying with the uncoverted down in the hall. Kneeled at the benches, read, prayed. The soldiers up on the dais sang in the meantime, keeping up the excitement. The guitar jingled. The groanings in the hall penetrated the music. In the half gloom it was almost impossible to see anything, except that several were leaning forward from the benches. These were the people who were moaning.

The prayer intensified. It went on and on. All the saved were praying. Burning, raving. O Jesus Our Saviour! Look upon the sinner, let him come to you! O let him come now, now this evening! O save a soul this evening! O before we part let a soul be saved! O and we shall sing your praises! O Jesus! O let us not have held this meeting in vain! O open heaven for a sinner this evening!

They went on and on. The whole room was heated, the air felt heavy, intolerable.

Anders sat pale, overstrained, with gleaming eyes – he was gasping, his chest heaving. As if he were about to join in and moan too! Start screaming! He wanted to . . .

He clung to the bench . . .

A little in front of him the young salvation officer lay praying with a worker's wife. He caught a glimpse of her face. Saw she was quite calm. She wasn't worked up, like him. Why not?

Quietly with clasped hands, she lay whispering. Perhaps praying, perhaps only talking – it wasn't possible to hear. Her mouth was moving, but it couldn't have been for any strenuous words, that could be seen. Everything about her was simple and ordinary. Her boots protruded beyond the bench, her skirt was a little crumpled. Only the red band on her hat burned like a flame above her.

They begged and prayed. Sang and sang – the same over and over. They groaned on the benches, sighed, agonized. They sweated their souls out, the whole room felt full . . . the arch pressed down, the walls pressed in, trapped, no way out . .

Eventually someone let himself go forward, a young man, staggered as if sleep-walking up in the light, drooped by the railing, cried out that he was saved, his face was jaded, empty, expressed nothing, just gawped, then he began to rave, the words cascaded . . . They rejoiced and sang! The guitars jangled. Glory and Honour! All Praise! Thanks be to Jesus! They took up the collection. Sang again. Thank you Jesus! Honour and Praise! At last it was over. Anders hurried out. Across the yard, out on the street, he was first away.

Turned his collar up, walked to and fro. Would wait for her.

What he felt was horrible. Complete disgust. And a freezing chill within him, a rancour against all that could want to impose upon him . . . The audience came thronging out, old hags, ugly young women who dragged their feet, boys who hung about sneering, mad Johan and the fellow who'd been saved . . . He thought they were stifling. Crept over to the other side so as not to be seen, felt ashamed to be waiting.

When the street was empty she came. In her uniform – what did she want to go around dressed like that for!

They walked out of town, along the country road that led eastwards, as they usually did. The weather had lightened, the sky had cleared and when they came into open countryside the moon shone out.

He could see her. Her face was quite distinct.

He asked how she could come upon the idea of joining the Salvation Army. She told him. They were so many at home, seven children and she was the oldest. There wasn't enough to live off and she had to go out. But she wasn't strong, as one had to be if one were to serve others. It could happen that she'd simply collapse from tiredness. But then she'd been saved, and since then she'd never felt that way again . . .

If she believed? Yes of course she believed! Jesus had taken her to himself. That evening, she'd never forget it! Yes, she was saved, of course she knew. And nothing is so wonderful as knowing that. But it was also good that she was secure, that she was provided for, had food, and clothes they got too from the Army. If there was something they specially needed, they could apply, and usually they got it. Things were much better for her now than they had ever been. She'd put her life in God's hands. But she would have preferred to have stayed at home with her mother and sisters and brothers, if she could, if she'd been able to support herself there.

Anders listened. Her hat hid her face as they walked beside each other talking. But her voice, that was her too. – That, then, was her story.

She said everything so simply and quietly. How did

she manage?

They came down to the lake. Crossed the narrow-gauge railway that follows the shore-line. There were no trains as late as this, it felt empty as it always does at a railway crossing when there is nothing to be seen but the track vanishing in both directions. But a linesman was on his way home in the darkness, his trolley could be heard further and further away into the forest.

Near the lake the road became muddy, her galoshes began to stick. They had to walk on the grass verge, close together. He felt the warmth from her, and her breathing . . . and her frail hand in his. They walked silently for some time. – Did he perhaps love her?

Carts came towards them, a whole line of them. The tired horses hung their heads, the men sat as if asleep. They were the herring-criers up from the coast, over sixty miles away, coming for the market tomorrow. With food-pack and spirit-flask beside them they slept up there above the herring that glinted behind their backs in the moonlight.

It was late. They had to turn here. But they stopped and looked at the lake for a little. Suddenly it was very bright. The moonlight fell directly on her. Her face was transfigured, her whole body. Once again she shone, and the worn stuff of her cloak seemed part of the light, as before. Light pouring round her, as if it were revealing her.

He stood looking as if he were in love with her. But there was a total purity about her. Her features paled, as if they weren't earthly – but without being spiritualized in ecstasy, in vehement suffering, in exultation. They were quite calm.

There seemed to be nothing of the animal in her. Why not?

He suddenly felt there was something oppressive in this very purity and goodness and in the light surrounding her. Thought he recognized it. She must be like something he'd already met . . .

There was something terrible in certain people because it reminded one of perfection, a desire to encompass certainty, perfect peace. When one met this, it simply made life more desolate. It gave a sudden warmth to life which life didn't possess and which simply made living harder, much heavier.

Had they been standing there for long? They ought to be going home.

They hurried into town. He felt as if he wanted to slip away from her. Or start talking blasphemously about what she believed in, tear down something for her. But they walked in silence.

The streets were empty. He saw her to the smithy. There was an extension behind it, a hovel where she lived. He felt it distasteful to be standing there by the wall behind which they howled and bellowed. They parted. She went into the house as if it were a human dwelling.

As if liberated from something he set off on his way home.

So ended the first years of his youth in mere disintegration, dishonesty, bewilderment.

Father and I

Father and I

When I was nearly ten years old, I remember, Father took me by the hand one Sunday afternoon and we set off for the forest to hear the birds singing. We waved goodbye to Mother, who was staying at home to make supper and couldn't come. The sun shone warmly and we went on our way briskly. All that about bird-song we didn't take so seriously, as if it were something specially fine or remarkable, we were healthy and reasonable people Father and I, brought up with nature around us, accustomed to it, no fuss. It was just that it was Sunday afternoon and Father was free. And we walked along the railway line, where other people weren't allowed to go, but Father worked on the railway and had a right to be there. This way we came directly into the forest, didn't need to go round the long way.

Both the bird-song and all the other forest noises began at once. In the bushes there was a twittering from finches and willow warblers, house-sparrows and song-thrushes, all the hum and babble that surrounds one the moment one steps into the forest. The ground was dense with white anemones, the birches had just broken into leaf and the spruces had fresh buds, there were scents from everywhere, beneath it all the forest floor lay steaming under the sun. Much ado all around us, bumble bees emerged from their holes, midges whirled round damp hollows, and from the bushes the birds would shoot out to snap them up and dive back down again just as quickly. Right enough a train came chuffing along and we had to step down the embankment. Father greeted the engine-driver with two fingers to his Sunday hat and the driver returned the salute with outstretched hand, everything at full speed. And so we tramped further on our way, on the sleepers that lay sweating out their tar in the glare of the sun, smells from everything, axle-grease and saxifrage, tar and heather pell-mell. We took big strides so as to step on the sleepers and not on the stone chips, which were rough and would wear out our shoes. The rails gleamed in the sun. On both sides of the track stood telephone poles and they sang as one walked past. Yes, it was a fine day. The sky was absolutely clear, not a cloud to be seen, nor should there be on such a day as this, according to Father. After a time we came to a field of oats, on the right-hand side of the track, where a crofter we knew had a piece of cleared land. The oats had come up dense and even. Father observed it with the mien of a connoisseur and it was clear he was pleased with what he saw. I didn't understand so much of things like that, for I was born in the town. Then we came to the bridge across a stream where there wasn't usually much water, but today it was running full. We held hands so as not to fall down between the sleepers. It wasn't far then to the little linesman's place that lies quite submerged in greenery, apple trees and gooseberry bushes; we went in to say hullo and were offered milk and saw their pig and their hens and their blossoming fruit trees, and then we carried on. We were going as far as the big river, for it was more beautiful there than anywhere else, there was something special about it, for further inland it ran past father's childhood home. We usually preferred not to turn back before reaching the river, and so today too we got there, eventually. It was nearly as far as the next station, but we didn't go that far. Father only saw that the signal was as it should be, he thought of everything. We stopped by the river. The current rumbled broad and friendly in the glittering sun, along the banks hung the spreading leafy trees, mirroring themselves in the slack water, everything was bright and fresh here, from the little lakes further up came a mild breeze. We clambered down the embankment and walked a little along the river-edge. Father pointed out the fishing places. Here as a boy he had sat on the stones waiting for perch, days on end, often in vain, but it was a blessed existence. He had no time now. We messed around for quite a while there, launching bits of bark on the current and throwing stones into the water to see who could throw furthest, we were by nature cheerful people, both Father and I. But at last we felt tired and decided we'd had enough, and set off on our way home again.

Then it began to gloom over. The forest was changed, it wasn't dark in there yet but almost. We hurried. Mother would no doubt be restless now, waiting with the food. She was always afraid something would happen. Nothing had. It had been a splendid day, nothing had happened other than it should have done. We were happy with everything. It darkened more and more. The trees were so strange. They stood listening to each step we took as if they hadn't known who we were. There was a glow-worm beneath one of them. Down there in the darkness it lay staring at us. I clenched Father's hand, but he didn't see the strange light, was just striding ahead. Darkness had fallen. Now we came to the bridge over the stream. It was roaring down there, horribly, as if it wanted to swallow us, the abyss opened right under us. We stepped cautiously on the sleepers, held hands rigidly so as not to tumble down. I thought Father would carry me across, but he said nothing, he doubtless wanted me to be like him and think nothing of it. We carried on. Father was walking there in the darkness so calmly, with even steps, without saying anything, absorbed in his own thoughts. I couldn't understand how he could be so calm when it was so gloomy. I looked around, frightened. It was just darkness everywhere. I scarcely dared take a deep breath, for then one took so much darkness in it could be dangerous, I thought, then one would soon die. I can well remember thinking so, then. The embankment sloped down abruptly on each side, as if into abysses black as night. The telephone poles rose like ghosts against the sky, a dull rumbling inside them, as if someone were talking deep down in the earth, the white porcelain insulators sat crouched and scared and listening. Everything was horrible. Nothing was right, nothing real, everything out of the ordinary. I drew close to Father and whispered: 'Father, why is it so horrible when it's dark?'

'No, dear child, it's not horrible,' he said and took my hand.

'But it is.'

'No, you shouldn't think so. For we know there's a God.'

I felt so lonely and abandoned. It was so strange that only I was afraid, not Father, that we didn't think the same. And strange that what he said didn't help me, that it was no use saying I didn't need to be afraid any more. Not even what he said about God helped me. I thought He too was horrible. It was horrible that He too existed everywhere here in the darkness, down beneath the trees, in the rumbling telephone poles – that was certainly Him – everywhere. And yet one could never see Him.

We walked in silence. Each thinking his own thoughts. My heart seemed to shrink as if the darkness had come in and had begun to squeeze it.

Then, when we were halfway round a curve, we suddenly heard a huge thundering behind us! We woke out of our thoughts terrified. Father pulled me down the embankment, down into the abyss, held me there. Then the train careered past. A black train, lights out in all the carriages, it was going at a furious speed. What sort of train was that, there shouldn't be any train just now! We watched it in astonishment. The fire glared in the huge engine where they were shovelling coal, the sparks poured wildly out into the night. It was dreadful. The driver stood there, pale, motionless, his features as if paralysed, lit up by the fire. Father didn't recognize him, didn't know who he was, he was just staring straight ahead, as if he were just going straight into the darkness, which had no end.

Overwrought, panting with anguish, I stood and watched the wild sight. It was swallowed up by the night. Father took me up to the track again, we hurried homewards.

'That was strange,' he said, 'what train was that? And I didn't recognize the driver.' Then he just walked in silence.

But I was trembling over my whole body. It was all for me, for my sake. I suspected what it meant, it was the anguish to come, all the unknown, what Father knew nothing of, what he wouldn't be able to protect me from. For this world, this life, would not be for me as it was for Father. Where everything was secure and known. It was no real world, no real life. It was only careering, burning, into the total darkness which had no end.

from *Onda sagor* (1924)

The Difficult Journey
Guest of Reality Part II

The Difficult Journey

When he was grown up Anders went away from his own country and came to another one. It was unlike his own. More luxuriant, richer, lay as if fermenting with well-being. Dense leafy woods oozed over the edges of the flat islands like dough on a baking-board; inland the whole countryside was cultivated, rich acres free of stones luxuriated, wheat-fields for more bread than the people could possibly eat, thriving farms with gorged farmers, cattle with bulging udders swaying between their legs. Everything was put to use, nothing was left untouched. The woods were parks, you could not walk in under the trees without stepping on sandwich papers. Nature was loved there as in few other countries, never left in peace, was something remarkable for everyone to gape at, even the farmers stared at it. There was something idyllic about it, which they loved, a sugary idyll covered the whole land. And people glowed with well-being and cosiness. They had a smooth joviality, shared, strangely, by widely differing types and classes, a round everyday-ness that unfailingly kept them going. They were comfortable. The world went their way. They seemed to take life as the most obvious thing that had ever happened to them.

A city which was much too big for the country sucked people in from all directions, chewed them and sent them back. Nearly everything had been chewed-over. Life there was a throng of *petit bourgeoisie* and culture, cosy comfort and soft degeneracy. It was a kind of richness, it seemed to him as he came from his own country, just as fat seems richer than thin. And life had a lightness, an informality, as if it thought of loosening you up, making more of you. He was drawn there perhaps because what he most lacked was there. Relished being away from his own milieu? But everything round about repelled him. And at the same time he enjoyed it. But in his own way. He well knew that this country and its people were not as he made them out to be, or at least that they were much else as well. Even so, he saw what he chose to see and picked out what were to him the most unattractive features and took pleasure in the lack of pleasure. He realized that his distaste for the country was the other side of his love for it, his love for the fair and happy and unconstrained. He admired those strange people who lived without more ado, lived just like that. It was only that he detested them. But this certainly meant a great deal for him, much more than he wanted to admit. In all this lack of style there lay a true humanity – but this was something he was not yet equipped to understand.

In the spring the city people rushed out towards the coast as if seized by the idea of drowning themselves, but remained contentedly paddling at the edge, revelling in the close-packed crowd on their strip of beach and cultivating their erotic connections. Anders found himself in one of the hundred boarding-houses along the coast. It was patronized by the middle-classes, officials and independent gentlemen and their families, stout wholesale-merchants in coffee and butter, and rolling matrons everywhere. The tiniest boxroom full from floor to ceiling, jovial crowding on stairways and in porches, on plush sofas and on verandas, chatting and cosiness, they stuck to each other like snails, with their whole being, and their husbands' and their children's lot since birth, their parlours in town, their flower-pots and nice pictures – and all in despair over not having known each other before now. Even far away from the house there could be heard a purling as from an eel-trap, stuffed to bursting and wobbling on the beach when it is set up and its contents writhe inside it. Fattened matrons manoeuvred themselves out through the glass doors on the balconies as if the panting house strained the plumpest of them out in order to avoid splitting at the seams.

Three times a day the whole establishment oozed with the smell of food and all the matrons waddled famished to table. Everyone sat together and there they were on display, bolting down food that swam in butter and fat, greasy and over-cooked, deprived of its taste. There were hardly any young people there, only ladies beyond a certain age, of which this country had fattened up a certain type, swelling with life, with gigantic bosoms and corsettes wide as troughs, arms smacking like thighs, hands loaded with rings, as if they were pensioned-off coquettes. Half of them had the straw-yellow hair which so often there gives a charming blondness to the children and the young but on those past their prime it can look tallowy, as if stuck to the scalp, above the lard-like face sweaty with talk and pleasure. They talked now not as earlier, but in a kind of rage, to and fro across the table, sharing everything, sharing themselves with everyone, exchanging fatty heart for roast while trying to score points off each other. Their breasts hung over the table, their faces were red and bloated with cutlets, sauce and beer, their armpits were wet with sweat as they gesticulated. Under the tablecloth it reeked of fat legs, sticky feet and the smell of a woman who did not keep herself clean. The chairs creaked beneath sheer mountains of flesh. Clearly the only thing to do was to run off and without saying goodbye jump into the sea and drown oneself.

Puffing and full-up they rose at last. Their summer dresses, neat and youthful and girlish, stuck to their shanks and did not blow free until they emerged in the open air.

Later, they could be seen again in the surrounding countryside. Obesely they trundled along in their carriages, gazed at woodlands drowsing to no purpose in the sunshine, dusty far into their thickets because of the cars on the roads that traversed them. There were people behind every bush. If there was a patch of grass it would be flat from people sitting on it. If the grass tried to rise again it would hear the tramp of new arrivals coming to sit down. And in the gardens round the boarding-house they lay distended on deckchairs and sofas, crawled into the shade of stout old trees, while the sea gurgled sluggishly at the edge of the shore.

It was in this enclosure of plump greenery and flesh that he met the woman he came to love. She stood out from the rest, that was immediately obvious. There was something wild and untutored about her, like an animal from the real forests in this herd of feeding sows. Her nature had something angular, a lack of charm which, when one perceived her as she really was, gave her a kind of charm in spite of herself. What was captivating about her was that she seemed to be so directly alive, an impression which so few of the living really give. It could be seen in her eyes, beautifully open, unclouded, ready for life. They could be so wonderfully exposed, and her mouth could have a tender sensitiveness when she sat in a serious or downcast mood. But suddenly, with a nervous impulsiveness, often without visible cause, something hard would appear in her glance, something defiant, cold, repelling. Although very young she had a bitter and aggrieved side to her nature, an almost raw unfeelingness in her judgement of people and the world as she saw them. There was something evil and inhuman in her. He felt that she was one of those who find it hard to love, to love properly and completely. But that this had no particular cause, it was just something in her, unelucidated. When it insisted on expression she was left there helpless, as if it were nothing after all. She was like an injured child unable to explain herself, able only to look bad. One wondered if that was her self, her essence, or if it came from outside, through some experience driving her in that way. In her fresh and slender frame she seemed in a sense broken, stunted in her growth. She was like a snapped tree that continues to grow, putting out wild shoots, raw and violent, without balance, away from the stem, hanging out over the edge.

They were drawn to each other. Not out of sympathetic attraction yet in order to come closer, as if groping towards whatever repelled them from each other, whatever prevented them from being indifferent to each other. There was no familiarity between them. From the very first they were constantly tense, on guard. If they opened up it was not to give, to speak from the heart; if they kept silence it was not to receive, to try to understand. And if some weakness emerged in what they managed to disclose, they broke off in dejection – for they then felt an emptiness, a lack of responding warmth, because the other had once already been rebuffed when something was revealed and the rancour was still there. For they had already hurt each other before they even knew who it was they met.

Hilde talked about her life. Not all at once, and not directly or open-heartedly, but with a pretence of indifference, as if it hardly mattered to her. Soon he could see, though, how her life had really been, including the parts she hid. What she tried to hide emerged most clearly of all.

She had grown up as an only child in a well-to-do home where nothing seemed to be lacking. It took some time for him to realize that something had in fact been lacking. Everything she could have wanted she had had; her childhood she remembered as piles of toys, fine clothes, a big garden loaded with flowers and fruit, with swings in the maples solely for her use, rose-bushes that were hers, lawns where she could run about, arbours in which to hold parties, unknown children standing at the gate sucking their fingers. The house was full of guests, people coming and going. Like an everlasting party. In this she lived, had everything.

Once when she was small, she remembered, she

had gone home with a playmate, into the kitchen. They had been running around and were now warm, so they went in to ask for some water. The little girl was rather dirty and wore patched clothes, she was someone she had met up with out on the road, someone she would probably not have been allowed to play with. But the moment they were inside the door the mother took up the red-cheeked bundle on her knee, hugged and kissed her, wiped some dirt off her face and kissed her again. Hilde stood beside them. It was like something that stung in her breast –

No one ever did that to her.

After that she always felt the same sting when she saw such things. She became a little bigger and mixed more with other children. Such things indeed seemed to happen often. She had a little playmate, who regularly clambered up on her mother's knee and the two of them would wrap their arms round each other. Hilde watched, said nothing, indeed there was nothing to say. But she would place herself beside them, right beside them, so close that she seemed to belong. She remembered always doing that when she was really small. But later, she recalled, she would stand aside a pace or two, without properly knowing why. She felt something uncomfortable was happening – stood waiting for the girl impatiently; couldn't she just come now and start playing!

Ever since the first time she felt such a sting she had carefully observed how things were at home – how Father and Mother were, how she herself was. She tried to feel how she felt. And how home felt. It seemed to her that she started this when she was quite small, was forced into it. Mostly it was her mother she watched in this way – each word, each expression, everything she did. She kept her under constant observation. Father was old, a distinguished man well on in years for whom she had an infinite respect and devotion. He had no time for her, gave her everything she asked for and was always friendly. Mother was middle-aged, almost young, a cold beauty everyone gathered round. She seemed able to attract anyone she chose to – at least among the men – yet it was a dead kind of coolness round her, surely they felt that, didn't everyone feel that? If she crept past while guests were in she could hear how her mother sat there in intimate conversation, with a strange lively cordiality, how she laughed – it sounded like someone else, not her. Her glance too had something tense in it, even when radiant, in her eyes there was something unsettled, they were opaque, no one saw who she was.

The little girl kept watch. Followed her, never let her go, thought and thought about her. She felt drawn to her, as well, like the others – after all, she was her mother.

That her mother was indifferent to her she noticed in everything. She was left to the servants or to herself. Yet she was the only little being here who ran about in the house, in the garden, and she had long blonde curls that tumbled out when she ran – she was brimful of life. Her little head brooded and brooded over this, that her mother did not care for her little girl. That Mother let her walk past – many many times in the course of the day she would walk past without her mother stretching out a hand or calling her. She never did that unless it was to correct her, to chide her for something.

But would she have wanted it? Would she have

wanted her mother to caress her? No. And that was what was so terrible. That she knew it would repel her – the very thing she longed for. She did not want it. Sometimes when people were there Mother would draw her close to herself, with pretended fondness – and that was why she knew this was something she did not want. She found it unpleasant and nauseating.

No, she felt indeed no love for her mother, had never felt any. She seemed to remember how once when she was very small she ran to her mother, as children do, only to be pushed away. But she could not properly remember if she had really done that. Perhaps she had never done such a thing.

Not to love her own mother! That was what she brooded over at an age when children should not be thinking about anything. It dug deep into her, dug a hole somewhere in her, just an empty hole which nothing ever filled.

She began to hide away. First down in the garden where she occupied a corner which she allowed to become unkempt, not so fine and tended as everywhere else. There she took bits and pieces, stakes that she made into a fence, bunches of twigs to fill the gaps so that no one could see in, boxes in which she had snails, tins with pupae and larvae, beetles and flies, a tortoise she had been given, a big tub of water full of tadpoles from a pool in the wood. There she would sit crouched over her little creatures, watching them, hanging over them for hours on end, no one knew where she was. These creeping things – they too had no one who cared for them. Pupae were found in rotten tree-stumps, larvae hung dangling in their slime on some leaf. No one bothered whether or not they turned into butterflies. The tadpoles scrambled over each other in the muddy water, searched for food, ate up those who had starved to death. If they were to turn into frogs they would have to manage by themselves. She sat there on a stool surrounded by her crawling mites and observing their behaviour, turning them over and watching how they righted themselves. If she caught a glimpse of someone out in the park she would keep absolutely still, creep further in. If it was her mother she would spy on her through a special hole, lurking and scrutinizing.

Later, when she was bigger, she took to wandering in the wood, long aimless walks alone with her dog. The dog bumbled along, right beside her, she always wanted to have animals with her. She would walk quickly, and preferably in the evening. There she would go, mulling over her life – like a fate, the way grown-ups feel. Working herself up with thoughts she could not sort out – about Mother, it always came back to that, for that was something which never received an explanation.

Now it had occurred to her that Mother told lies to old Father. Why did she? Constantly and consistently, over small things that meant nothing, and then too in matters where Father ought to have known, things which one did not talk about, or for which there were ready-made phrases. For one ought to be obliging the maids too, everyone in the household, the kitchen people included. 'It was a shame about Father. He was also lonely, outside in a way, no one bothered about him either.'

Mother bothered about everyone. It felt like a constraint. She bound everything with her will – and yet, this was the strange thing, she had no will. It did not feel as if she wanted anything, it was often clear that she did not, there was a vacant wandering restlessness in her, inside an icy shell. She radiated only a coldness, it could be sensed perpetually. She herself could be sensed, always. One could be sitting there and feel 'Now she's coming.' Alerted by a strange discomfort, one could know that she was in the next room, one could tiptoe to the door and look out and there she stood. She was always being sensed in this way. Everyone felt it. No one could properly free themselves from her. As for Father, yes, he did love her.

Hilde thought she felt only hate. And still she longed for her, because she was her mother. Often when she was not directly thinking about her but yet aware of her as being there in a less direct way, as being someone close to her, she realized she was in fact longing without wanting to.

She had reached the age when a girl needs a certain intimacy with her mother, when they come to meet in a new way and when restlessness can be stilled by a new warmth growing between them. She had had to do without that before, for that very reason perhaps needed it less than others, still, she could not help longing for it again. She could sit down out in the wood and weep – as if for Mother? It could hardly be for Mother. She wept anyway, without knowing why.

No, Mother wanted nothing of her. The mere idea of turning to her, of needing her in any way, put an end to the weeping and she felt hard and cold, began walking again, faster than before, her mouth clenched. One ought to be like Mother. Untouched, refusing to let anyone come close, that was right – Just like mother. That was how she wanted to be. She saw her as she was.

But Mother – was she really sure of herself? She seemed to be, with others, but not when alone, not if she were to walk here in the wood and think about something, anything, but she would not want to do that. Perhaps would not dare.

There was something peculiar about her gaze. If one watched her eyes without her being aware of it, they were restless and wandering, never rested on anything. It was only when they looked directly at one that they became firm and steady, not otherwise. And dignity which never left her was tense and lifeless, as if she held herself up. She seemed to be eaten away from inside, in danger of collapsing. And around her there could be felt the same insecurity, it spread out from her although she appeared so calm and controlled. The whole household was like her. It felt as if it were dissolving in decay, though from the outside that was not apparent. Those who simply came and went were probably unaware of it. And Father – he noticed nothing.

Hilde also paid attention to something else in her mother which seemed strange. At times she could be altogether radiant with high spirits, not in any natural way but with a kind of restrained exhilaration, and at times she appeared only lethargic and apathetic. She tried to conceal both moods, especially if Father was at home, but clearly she did not always succeed.

Hilde did not remember when it was she came upon the explanation for this and of course for much else. She thought at first her mother drank, for she had seen her doing so at dinner parties and had observed how she changed in the process. Later she found out that it was morphine she had fallen to. This discovery stirred up everything within her, all her obscure feelings. She would have liked to weep, really weep, in despair – she was after all her mother. She was sorry for her, something must after all have driven her to it, something difficult, maybe one should not judge her too harshly. She would have liked to stroke her on the cheek, to try to help poor Mother. At the same time she felt a certain satisfaction that this is how things were. That she really was so degraded, right down, at the bottom. And that she, Hilde, had pried out the secret. No one had bluffed her. She had seen through Mother long ago, understood how she was, understood something was not right with her. And now she had come upon this. How many others would know? Not many. Not the maids and not the people who came about the house. They thought Mother was a perfect creature, admired her, looked up to her. Perhaps there was no one who knew? Father? He did not know.

Now she had something to hold to. She developed an interest in her mother's depravity which was abnormal, which distorted everything in her, which half blinded her, twisted her youth just as her childhood had been twisted. She watched her mother constantly. She observed the effects, what condition her mother was now in, how it changed and how she kept herself going, how she tried to hide. How she conceived of herself, how she made herself sick, all the methods she used to get hold of what she must have. And her immorality, falsehoods, wastefulness, how she let everything go to pot. How the home was decaying, as if eaten away from inside, looked well-to-do from the outside and was well-to-do no longer, how the silver vanished from the cupboards, the piles of linen shrank, no one knew where things went. She observed everything. She was perpetually alert. She was consumed by her interest in watching everything in a state of disintegration.

It half blinded her too when she observed others, when she looked at other circumstances and into other homes – the process spread out. She saw only rottenness everywhere. Only disintegration, decay, ambiguous personalities, lies, pretence, and in everyone a cold calculating way of reaching one's own ends. She saw only Mother. And she thought that this taught her how the world was. It seemed to her to give the key to human beings, so that she could enter them. It paid off, she came upon so much.

As far as Mother was concerned she was right. She saw that, and so she believed that she was always right, since she had been right in the case of Mother. For she could follow the whole course of her misery, how it developed. She saw how in secret she was sinking deeper and deeper, she seemed to glide down imperceptibly. There was a certain excitement in witnessing this, Hilde never tired. Coldly and impassively she observed how Mother became more and more repelling.

At times she shied back in terror at the idea of really despising and loathing her own mother. How was such a thing possible? How could such abnormality exist? Surely she had other feelings for her? Hadn't she? Yes, she felt her heart was so full of. . . but it must have been something else. She would have liked to weep for her, really weep. . . she wanted to be good to her, wanted in some way to help her.

But she was worth only loathing and contempt! Nothing else. It was Mother who was inhuman, unnatural.

How did she get hold of what was corrupting her?

That doctor who was always around the house, what about him? Did he know? Was there something between him and Mother?

And other men who came to the house – what was there between them and Mother? Was there someone she had a special feeling for, someone she perhaps loved? Someone she wanted to come, someone she sat and waited for? Someone with whom she talked quietly? Someone with whom she wanted to be really close – someone she is perhaps going out to meet now? One person she was really fond of? One person always in her thoughts?

It was strange – Hilde never found an answer to such questions. Did not know what to believe. Understood nothing. On this matter Mother was inaccessible. She disclosed nothing. Not with a gesture, not with a word. The matter was closed, incomprehensible.

Hilde thought about this a lot because she was now at the stage where she began to have the first stirrings of love. It felt strange, it was she felt so hard to hold back, to keep hidden. Surely it showed? She did not want it to be seen! But her heart was so full . . .

No, she did not think her mother could love, not properly. She let no one close enough, never gave herself. Perhaps did not dare to. No doubt she was frightened of Father although she did not care about him. And she was desperately anxious about her reputation, as if it were the only thing she possessed. No, she could not love. She took, she absorbed, because she wanted to, perhaps because she counted this as an advantage – she had no thought of giving in return. In an inexplicable manner she exploited her ability to captivate . . . It was terrible. It could startle one. And still, Hilde more or less admired her mother when she thought about it. It captivated and held her. To be able to remain so untouched, to control both herself and others, to twist everything to her will with power which one kept hidden, let no one suspect. It was like living in stealth, without ever letting it break through or out. Perhaps one ought to be like that. Never show one's feelings, not even feel them properly – not even for oneself. That was perhaps the right way to live.

Hilde could not live like that. She lay sniffling up in her room, all alone. Her tortoise scratched about under the sofa, the parrot she had been given when she was small sat there jabbering some words it had copied from the little girl when she had trained it to speak. Hilde buried her head as deep in her pillow as she could. Something was hurting her, really hurting her. She was healthy and helpless in spite of everything she had understood and seen. She was not at all what one should be, not yet. She could feel that clearly enough, and it hurt a lot.

Her mother suddenly acquired a strange interest in her, an interest she had never shown before. She wanted to sit and talk, or she wanted to go out and take a walk. She was on the track of her heartache, nosing, to find out where it would lead. And she got her to be open about it, to confide. To Mother! It was incomprehensible. Hilde did not understand how it was possible. Did not understand how she came to respond. It happened without her suspecting anything. She had a way of trapping people so that they forgot themselves and for the moment had no wish to be suspicious. She would throw out a few questions, would give the impression that she could help, if one said something, told her how things were. And so she found out what she wanted.

She knew how to pry. How to get hold of, find out about, anything when she wanted. And stealthily, without its being suspected, without anyone knowing about it.

Afterwards Hilde was full of shame. That she could confide in Mother! And now here she was sitting alone again. No one had given her any consolation.

Later, an easier time came. She became engaged and thought she was happy, often felt that she was.

Mother disapproved of the engagement, if not openly then secretly. There were scenes, repeatedly, without apparent cause, and the daughter would come off worse. Mother incited Father too, told lies about her, things that were unreasonable and had never happened. She felt hated and rejected. But everything here was now falling apart. The home was like a desert, or a ruin, no one came any more, no guests, everyone could see what it was like. Perhaps old Father as well, who was now at the edge of the grave.

The engaged couple began to drift apart. Their engagement crumbled, like everything else. Hilde went about tear-stained, red-eyed again, hid herself away. Mother watched her, it felt as if she knew everything. She kept close, always, like a vulture watching something dying. But she was a little more friendly, as if sorry for her – that was repulsive. Hilde disclosed nothing, said nothing, just came and went. She was walled-in.

Then one day it was over, properly. It felt hard and

cruel although she herself was to blame. She had come home afterwards in the evening and the others were sitting at dinner. At last she could hold out no longer, jumped up and made for the sofa, threw herself down and burst into tears.

Mother sat and watched. Her slack face which was not young and not any longer beautiful took on a weird twisted expression that might have been of pain. It seemed dead, sunken. But she said nothing and did not come over. She just sat watching, her eyes dry and open and the small narrowed pupils staring over at the sofa. As if she was devouring the whole scene.

It was not long after this that the great event took place, the event which fell on Hilde like a stroke of lightning and threw its cold light everywhere, on everything, explaining and changing everything.

She found out that Mother was not her mother. And Father not her father. They had adopted her when she was small because they could not have children of their own and because the house felt empty, the young wife wanted to adopt a child, as if she wanted something with which to distract herself. But perhaps she longed for a child too, no one could know. She was not much more than a child herself, and she had the baby as a doll, fussed over her, dressed her up in the finest lace and linen, all the sweetest little drolleries, delightedly showed her off to the whole world.

And then she had wearied of her. She had thrown herself into the life of parties and entertainments, made the most of her position by the side of her ageing husband and the child had simply become a nuisance. People did not know everything about her.

Only that she had become as she was, and the house like her. The child remained. She could well have got rid of the child, but that was not possible, seeing she had already been adopted. The child grew up there in the house, left to herself. That is how things turned out.

Hilde felt as if a weight had been lifted from her breast. She remembered how she went out walking in the town, walking and walking for hours. Burning inside. Seized by wild joy. Yes – she had never been so glad. Wasn't she laughing? But her cheeks were chalky white. She walked up streets and down streets, to and fro, inflamed, everything within her seething and shut in.

'So *that's* how it is, *that's* how it is! That is life!'

How she remembered that afternoon! It was an ordinary day in early summer, the kind one usually says is beautiful. Sunny. She remembered how she saw everything in a sort of dead washed-out light, each house, each gable, each window, the paving-stones, each single object, quite drily and clearly. The signs, the advertisements, the passing cars, the passing faces, all in a light that was dead from its own sharpness, which cut into her eyes. And how she walked with her eyes wide open, imbibing the light, how she walked savouring the light.

Yes, that's what the world is like! That's life! Like this. Hard, cruel, raw, unnaturally evil. She had been right! She had seen correctly. Everything from the past rose before her, all of her poisoned childhood and youth, everything she had known throughout those terrible years. She had felt correctly. She had understood life as it is. She had seen quite correctly. Now she would see even more correctly, even more clearly, still more!

With that her story ended.

That was how she was. That was how her life had been.

Anders felt both gripped and repelled by what she told or allowed to be understood. He was gripped by this desperate picture of a home, it was something he could never forget and it filled his mind every time he thought about her. He saw his own home, his mother and father and the old people out on the farm – and what he had heard felt alien and repelling. But when he thought of his childhood and upbringing as it *really* had been, in spite of the warmth in which home had folded it, as it had existed within him and as he had really lived through it – then her story came strangely close, no matter how remote it seemed from his. He felt all the emptiness, desolation, anxiety striking him – and he recognized it. What filled his childhood and youth, the only thing that really was him, everything he had come through, in which he had always lived, and which through the following years had simply grown and grown, seized upon him more and more hungrily, deeper and deeper, until he was at breaking point, with a thin membrane separating him from the outer world, on the edge, unbearably sensitive to everything – for that was how he was when they met, at the limit of what he could bear of nervous excitement, of rancour towards life as he saw it, as it forced itself upon him. And he thought that what she had gone through represented this hated life as it was, laid it bare, unveiled all its rawness, represented it honestly, undisguised, naked, without a glimmer of goodness, reconciliation or warmth, which at heart it did not possess. He felt a raw breath strike him, a fresh bitterness – Things like this made it easier to live. One could breathe out, feel liberated . . .

And so they met.

They were both engrossed in, inflamed by, the same thing – and a gaping abyss lay between them. The same bitterness and sterile emptiness which brought them together lay wide open between them. He thought he had never felt such a gulf between himself and another human being, had never met anyone so difficult to share anything with, or to give anything to.

They did not reach each other. And they did not even try, they did not even stretch out from the edge, over the abyss – they just had it there always between them, something in common. It belonged to both of them, it was theirs.

It drew them to itself. It bound them. They could not get away, go where they pleased. They were compelled to walk along the edge, close to it. In a way close to each other, only emptiness between them – as if nothing separated them.

There was a ceaseless tension in this, something peculiarly stimulating. And it became something conscious, both of them knew about it. Felt as if they belonged together. Were in a sense fated to meet, and in this way.

Those strange walks they took together. They could not speak to each other about anything, not in any calm or controlled way. Not without it suddenly ending with some spiteful words thrown at each other, meaninglessly, they did not know where the words came from. And so they would walk in silence. What they did not do was part company. They never thought of that. They would have saved each from suffering, together, much pain and bitterness if they had parted company. But apparently they did not want to do that. Or could not.

He asked himself often enough why he was walking here with her, alongside her. Why? It only hurt, churned up everything. And it was the same for her. It was pointless, it gave them nothing. Often enough he saw the abyss lying wide open between them and her walking there on the other side – in one way close to him, in another way distant – so that he saw her clearly. She went up there like an animal, with a free and unaffected gait, yet out at the very edge. Then, when she was so young, newly become a woman, she had that unpremeditated gait which belongs to the animal.

They egged each other on, always walking like this, as if separated. There was something erotic in it too, in the way they could never really meet, in the way everything remained foreign although they secretly felt they belonged together. The reason no doubt lay in this mixture of sensations crowding in on them, which they could not hold apart. And in their perpetual watchfulness over each other – how they watched and watched! In the very rancour that kept breaking out between them there was something exciting, for they felt it driving them together.

Did they find anything to hold on to in each other? Nothing they knew of. Nothing to hold on to. But much that egged them on, drove them together. They seemed to be repelled by almost everything in each other – but it was as if they both had a desire for, an attraction towards what they found repelling.

There came a time when they said they loved each other. And in a way they told the truth. But it was a love without tenderness. It was not a love that built up anything for them. From the beginning it was as if determined that it would not be able to do so.

He saw how ill-fated and hopeless it was, the way they were drawn to each other. But he did not try to prevent it happening. He wanted it. During all this time he went around in a perpetual state of dull oppression – but violently alive underneath, as he always was when he felt pressure on him, when he felt his inner being tightening in a knot. When his life was shutting him in, walling him in, he was stumbling down in the cellar, groping his way ahead. It was then he lived most vehemently, with a sudden violence that felt liberating. There was emptiness and tension inside him, a desolation and over-excited eagerness which he recognized. He was in the ascendant, it was a time when he felt exhilarated and alive.

As a rule lovers come closer and closer to each other. They did, too. They winkled out each other's peculiarities and weaknesses, the contemptible or the ridiculous, everything that hides, they both had plenty of that. They stored up in their memories what was said, what was unsuspectingly revealed – and in due course much was revealed between them – in order to make use of it later. Nothing was overlooked, nothing was forgotten. Each little word that hurt came back. They learned to know where they could hurt. And where the old wounds lay, those not yet healed. It was as if nothing else occupied them. They could throw themselves at each other with a spitefulness that was unreasonable, quite without foundation. So far. – And still they hung together, could not let each other go. And in a way they hung well together. It felt like a kind of madness.

And around them the well–fed matrons swelled, waddled about in the sunshine, down the sandy paths with their slack flesh. Food smells floated out through the windows, across the lawns and the dense flowerbeds which had been planted so thickly that no earth was visible beneath. The trees bulged lazily over the water. Everything lay as if stupefied by comfort.

In the middle of this a butterfly came flickering around him, as often happened when he felt some inner compulsion tightening, when he wanted to sink further into his own self. He had noticed that before. And that life was never only one thing, at least not to him although it is only within one thing that we really live. As in a cleft that shuts itself, digs itself in, in the ground. And up above the clouds drift this way and that and morning comes and evening and we see the shifting time that is the life of everyone, that draws past us.

It was like a butterfly, flickering up out of the grass. Fair and light, risen from the land itself, blonde and smiling like the land that lay floating on the sea. She had the warmth and the sunny glitter that belonged to the temperament there, the good-humoured roguishness, the open-heartedness that rose from warmth. And over her when she came towards him, over her hair and skin, there was something golden, that belonged to the young women of that country.

They got on well together, when they came together much in them changed. They went about like children carefree as the sunny days surrounding them. In the soundless transparent summer night they would meet and watch through the short hours together, down by the sea which lay there motionless with its pale Nordic water – up in the trees the nightingales began, inside the tree-tops which seemed to light up with the song, the beaches were mirrors without darkness, unreal, as in the very stillness around them the land seemed without weight, floating. They would go and look at the edge of the shore, under the trees – the water went right in under them, under the earth where they stood. Her country really was lying floating on the sea, all the smiling islands.

Like a dream. They stood by each other, looking, as if at home with her. A land made in play, scattered from the Creator's hand on a summer night like this when He rested from his strenuous toils and smiled at His own severity – from that smile this land was made – long ago but on just such a night, an hour like now. And from the mainland in the south the heathery moors stretched out their rough arms, up towards his own land, towards the barren north, joining it, surrounding the blonde dream out here at sea.

They smiled together. Yes, like a dream, light-filled and happy.

He stood thinking about it and fell silent. This sort of thing could never really mean anything to him. But they were always cheerful together, that just happened by itself.

Once she asked why he felt drawn towards Hilde; he knew but did not understand. And something shone in her eye he had not seen there before.

He fell silent. They walked in silence for a long time, which was not their habit, it must have been the first time. At last he said that he could not explain it. That it was just like that. It felt as if they had spent a long time seeking each other.

One evening when the kitchen maid was standing at her window washing up her greasy dishes, they left, went over to his country. They came to a cottage at the foot of a steep hill that rose abruptly right behind it. There, the back of the house was unpainted, the three other walls, facing the farmland, were painted red. An old lady owned the place, she was poor and thin in an old tight bodice with gathered insets and long close-fitting sleeves, she always wore that, seemed frightened, when she spoke she could hardly be heard, she lived in the kitchen. In the two rooms there were a few pieces of furniture, some chairs and a couple of pull-out sofas where you could lie almost down on the floor. The wallpaper was dark and bulging, faded by damp in some places because the rooms would not be heated in winter, the house was half dilapidated. The garden outside was overgrown, the gooseberry bushes full of grass and stray oats gone to seed. Radish grew wild everywhere and rhubarb had spread over rubbish-heaps with several self-sown potato clumps.

But down from the cottage lay the wide-open countryside, fragrant with rye and clover, well tended and beautiful, and the hill above them was full of flowers, birch trees and hazel thickets wherever they went – hill after hill, all bright. It was in the middle of nature's brief period of revelation there in his country, when everything is adorned, every garden, every pasture, every path festooned with ox-eye daisies, every stone with mountain everlasting and birdsfoot trefoil. And the day has no ending and up in the hills there sparkles from morning to evening an invisible crown of birdsong.

Indoors, in their rooms, it was always shady

because of the apple trees and the hill, but outside it was always sunny, and if the windows were open all the scents came in. The ants had a roadway across the floor in one of the rooms, they crawled up by the fire-wall and made their way out over by the corner next to the kitchen. As long as the day lasted they crawled there in a steady stream, and the two humans got into the habit of stepping over them and sitting on the sofa watching them, how they struggled along, what they dragged with them. It was like living somewhere in the woods.

Here they spent a summer, Hilde and Anders. It suited them, both in there, with its dereliction, and everything outside. They wandered in the hills, and preferably out towards the sea which lay over there beyond the hills, the real sea running green and open like a host of all earth's vanished springtimes, lingering here as an imperishable lustre, an eternal April. They could hear it at night in their room where they lay keeping watch together. It was the only thing to be heard. The open windows gave on to the garden which no one tended, the farmland seemed to them remote. Outside and round about was empty. They knew no one there and no one knew them. Probably no one knew that they were living there, for no one was ever seen going up to the house, to which there was no road anyway. The house lay as if abandoned. And the rooms with their bare walls stood as if no one lived in them. It suited them here, as if they were comfortable. And their love was undisturbed, could grow as it wished.

It was a love almost without tenderness. A heat, not a warmth, not something which lingered or enveloped them or in which they lived together. It was like a wind they both walked directly into – just something open and hard, a raw air they walked together in, quickly so that it heated them up. It was so lacking in softness, so devoid of any fragility, that it was not worth its name. It did not seem as if they had any feelings for each other, none which they wanted to show. They did not give each other anything, they only took. But there was a certain openness and cleanness between them, a lustre of heedless springtime, a wide-awake intoxication of the senses which was only intensified by the lack of intimacy. It was like a healthy and perhaps rough piece of nature, an undisciplined field where all the blossoming life is generated one windy day, by a wind from far out at sea, freely, impetuously, in the open air. Not the kind that hangs on and fades away.

He felt it as a freshness he had never before felt, something he had longed for without knowing he did, it answered something deep within his self. He had loved and had been loved, but without it really meaning much to him, for it had never taken hold of what was really him. Had never dug in deeply. Had lain there unused, not worth anything. And he had to dissemble, pretend. Had to hold back so much that love became only a semblance of life alongside real life, a happy state of well-being that was not him, that oppressed him. Now for the first time he could give himself just as he was, without pretence, without the tenderness he did not want – that is how he felt – without the oppressive softness that creeps into the heart, but with something loveless in the middle of love itself holding it open around one, letting it be as itself. She bound nothing in him, as love binds, she gave without restriction. The excitement he lived in, without letting it be noticed, did not need to be smuggled out of the way, he did not have to lie about it to others, she took it and she gave it back. The rancour and dissatisfaction he went around with, did not need to be held back – it could flare up between them, like a fire given a blast of air. He did not have to pretend a happiness he did not feel, that he did not want, he did not need to pretend anything, only walk on beside the person he had met, without showing her any warmth – and still love her. For that he did.

We can go through long empty periods thinking that something decisive within, in our very being, is worthless and unusable for love. Something most deeply secretively our own – so we think, for we can be wrong as often as right, there is no knowing. That is what he had felt. He had never thought that this which kept itself hidden within him, which was obscured even from himself, would be of any use to love, would be laid bare by it. There is a humiliation in this, which weighs down our life more than anything. And it helps little that love clears other land within us, the humiliation remains, and what is forgotten can be sensed even more strongly because it is our own, just as we always feel the dead flesh but not the living – we do not notice the living flesh. If then love bursts in blindingly over this shady concealed corner, it feels like a violent liberation, a restoration, an intoxication without measure.

That was what he felt. Now everything he had carried within himself could break free, everything he had always held back, at home, during his upbringing, before those he met, out of some weakness in himself – now it could break free, raw, open, unconcealed, as it could only with a woman. He escaped from the oppressiveness, the vapours cleared. At last, so he thought, he stood there totally alive. But this that was laid bare was not something in which he could find any joy. He could not, knowing what he did. It repelled him, this that he had been plaguing himself with – he just wanted to see it set free. He did not want to hold on to it, felt bitter towards it, counted it worthless, even more so now that it had come to light. He had hidden it away. And so he felt no gratitude to her for digging it up. What should he be grateful for! She enticed out of him not something good, not anything that brought peace – *that* was something she could let lie! She just brought out everything else. Could he feel any joy or gratitude over that? Could he feel happy? It was only the sense of liberation he savoured.

He had never been like this towards any woman, she had certainly not ever been like this towards any man. They could not speak together in any way that suggested warmth, that suggested they were fond of each other, although they knew they were. They could not have a secure happy day together, never a whole one, perhaps for a while – more than that they seemed to grudge each other. Not even nature could they walk about in and enjoy calmly together, although they both loved it, lived in it as if at home in it and both of them found much peace in nature if they went alone. They started a habit of not walking together, for neither had any joy of their being together on such walks, they went off their separate ways. Then they would meet again towards evening, somewhere in the hills, and so keep each other company on the way back. If they saw each other too soon, before it was time to turn, they would avoid each other. And they accustomed themselves to walking in silence for whole days after throwing some rancorous words at each other, or even without doing so, because they had thought of something said before.

Those long summer days when they roamed around one by one, perhaps wanting to meet, perhaps not wanting to meet, for their wants fluctuated without their knowing why. Those fervid reconciliations when they drew together, when everything would be suddenly forgotten. Those nights when they made up to each other for all the goodness they had neglected, when they caressed as lovers do, rested beside each other in a happiness which did not seem to be theirs and which they would not refer to afterwards, not admit to having felt. The intoxication which carried them along, swept them away, and they thought only how they belonged to each other, for always, never could be separated, nothing could separate them, it only seemed so. The twilight when everything that had never been said was whispered. Then they would joke about how they were, about how they could carry on! All the joy that broke out filling the room, the whole summer night around them. The clover scent that drifted in through the windows, the rough sheets that felt damp, warm, the fresh smell of body. And then the rancour that could mix in with the excitement, into this love that was perpetually on the watch, for ever in wait, which did not want peace. They could lie beside each other in the darkness without talking, separated by a single word just after they had given each other everything, with open eyes, awake for hours, falling asleep through saying nothing. It was deathly still, the rooms were bare, naked as themselves, empty as if life had fled. They lay unmoving as corpses, like two lovers who had sought death, their love remaining around them as a deathly silent darkness, as an empty depth. – Then they could hear someone mumbling, humming away to herself behind the wall of the kitchen. It was not the old woman, another voice, weak and wailing, no coherence, like a sick child. They knew that both lay listening to it. And that neither knew what it was. For the old woman lived there alone, there was no one with her. When the voice began it could be heard as a continuous murmur. It sounded like a languid moaning, without despair and without any hope, without meaning, monotonous and slurred – no, it was not a child. They became ill at ease lying listening to it. They could often hear it right until they fell asleep.

One morning the old woman came and asked them if they had heard anything from her part of the house through the night. It was an insane daughter she had with her. She wanted to say so because she thought they might have been frightened. They should not worry about it. And if any time they should catch sight of her they should pretend not to see her. But she hardly ever went out.

Afterwards they did see her now and then in the evenings. She would be sitting up on the hill, outside an old privy which was wedged into a nook, she would be humming and singing away to herself. She was young but shrunk as an old woman, the untidy shale-grey hair hanging down round her dull lifeless face. Perhaps she had been sitting there before, without their seeing her. They thought they had heard someone singing somewhere above them as dusk gathered.

Hadn't they heard her from the very beginning? They pretended she was not there. And it seemed as if she did not notice them. She was not singing for them.

Summer lay brightly over the earth, their love blossomed in it, in its way. For love it was, a blossoming, something which lived. They were alive, they knew they were. Continuously alive. There was some purpose to their existence. It was something created and changing, something happening to them. And so in the middle of their turmoil it felt like something healthy. Life has many kinds of health, is not as twisted as one thinks, not even when it seems so. And this healthiness of theirs was not to be despised, they were drawn towards a real and direct life, careless of all else, of all pretence.

No one would have thought that they loved each other, although they certainly did. But they could not help being as they were. Every moment they were ready to expose each other, what the other was thinking right now, why the other was not saying something – as if each lived there in the other, not in himself or herself. And if they walked apart it was as if they were walking together. They could even feel closer then, than if they were walking side by side.

But there was no great happiness for them to live in. They made everything difficult and joyless for each other, as heavy to bear as they could. If one does not love then one can avoid much, cover up, arrange, keep things going. They avoided nothing. They exploited everything to the limit. Sought out what they could exploit. And that is how they wanted to live together. It arose too from that desire for discomfort which they both had. For them love itself was to be uncomfortable.

He had to tell himself that basically there was nothing in her that he did not love. He loved also because there was so much in her, both outwardly and inwardly, that he found repelling. He loved her lack of charm, which made passion more naked, laid love itself bare. He loved something coarse and over-simplified in her view of everything, in her attitude to life, a simplification which dragged life down and deprived it of the reverence which he himself needed to feel. He loved the way she drew a line over slighter or more sensitive perceptions, making it feel as if such things did not exist. He loved in her what made him suffer. What separated them, and in a fundamental way made them irreconcilable. He loved the fact that it was a totally different life that walked beside his own.

But this was something which he could only sense, and which could break out in passion. Otherwise it broke out in a strong distaste of her, an over-heated sensitivity to everything that repelled him, a perpetual violent assertion of himself, of the self he felt deep within, living a stronger and richer life, carrying on a more spiritual struggle than she was – and yet he always thought she was worth more than himself. He was split in two. He felt on two different levels, as love often lets us do, to torment us, and because it wants to divide everything living, wants decay and disintegration. He fought both with and against this force. He lived his two lives, meshed together, twisting into each other – did not know which one he was living.

Perhaps in this period he was in a state of unnatural excitement. But not so unnatural for him, for each of us has our own sense of balance and he did not feel so far from this. What is natural is nothing fixed, it fluctuates according to circumstances and we do not exceed the limits as readily as we think we do. He felt alive and strong, open to his life, ready, the only happiness there is. Both of them indeed felt like that. They stood open, ready for everything, without premeditation, nothing calculated, simply surrendering themselves. Facing whatever would impose on them, and resisting it. Like two men facing out a gale at sea. They felt life had grasped them, if only in order to tear them. They felt it grasped hard and rough, in earnest. They felt the joy of being young, of being able to expend themselves, of having the strength to feel as they did. They were much too alive, they wanted to miss nothing.

Neither of them was splendid or significant. That is no part of their story. What should they be? Isn't life still significant enough in itself? In the eyes of one of those who 'see through' people they would no doubt have been found quite empty and meaningless. They belonged to those who cannot be reached in that way. And that hardly bothered them. They just existed. For them the life they lived was a closed world – whether it was rich or poor, trivial or important, meant nothing to them. All that mattered to them was their ability to fulfil themselves, just as they were, and to be aware that they were doing so, to be unremittingly aware of their own lives. That ability had become extreme. There was something devouring, almost devastating about it. Behind lay something else – that for them life never felt obvious, it was a condition they simply found themselves in, they did not know how to cope with it. It was a matter of uncertainty and struggle in a big empty space, what else could they do but try to find themselves and each other, see if that would help them to understand what they were and why they were there and feel they were really doing so.

Did she feel that? Surely she did. For that was what she was like. Or was that just something he imagined? No, what she perhaps only guessed at, he *knew*. Often when he tried to explain to himself how they belonged together he thought that was part of the answer, it drew them together. They helped each other, clung together, could in a way use each other.

Hilde was truly a person who tried to live. He had felt that from the beginning and never forgot how moving that was. It was for her a question of life itself, not of adapting to its outer forms, fitting in with them – such as existence means for most people, and in the course of its struggle their very lives perish and they manage thus to avoid living. She did not want to avoid her life. It was the only thing she really owned. She had nothing else, only one life, something difficult and uncertain she was going to endure. Because of her home and upbringing she was rootless, without any base, without any tradition, only a being, something that existed – no one was better equipped than he was to see that, and no one better equipped to be moved by it, to experience it, she was not so bound hand and foot as he was. She was as abandoned and lonely as we all are, though life tries to pretend, tries to conceal it from us. Take away the disguise and there we see it. For him she was an image of Mankind – nothing else, just this helpless thing put into a world to live there. And she had lived awry, distorted from the beginning. She had been poisoned already by her childhood, which was hardly suprising. All life poisons us, that is not so strange, what else would it want with us, it secretly poisons us all. The very thing that makes us truly alive is a poison injected into us. He had nothing against asserting that, doing so did not make life heavier – on the contrary. Nothing raw or difficult made life unendurable – but everything else, everything that would reconcile us to it. Here there was no disguise, here everything was honest – and she lived honestly in the midst of it.

Strangely enough she had many features in common with her mother, who was not her mother. She seemed fresh, healthy, naïve – and yet inwardly she had something unnatural, an emptiness somewhere in her emotions which was never filled and which she did seem to care about having filled. Did she care about that? Then why was she the way she was? At heart she had a real living warmth – but she did not dare let it break out, it repelled her in a way, as if it would have meant exposing herself. She did not dare show her feelings, not even admit that she had them – everything good in her was hidden. There was, as he learned to know her, came closer to her, something appalling and stifling. One could not say, though, that she was evil. But she did have a leaning towards the malevolent, was drawn to it, she was drifting, with no hold on anything outside herself, in the things that help people, bind them together. It seemed that while she fought against her mother in order to be rid of her, in order to loathe her, cut all bands, she had come to resemble her, despite all the basic differences between them. The hatred towards her mother which she had to achieve was something she could not feel without the same unnatural qualities she met in her mother, she had to learn them, inject herself with them. She had to seek out everything within her that could help her in that direction.

And the mother was not her mother. The deepest unnaturalness lay in fact in the child, who hated in the belief that it really was her own mother she hated. The mother's crime was a cruel lack of feeling, a piece of dead flesh. But in the daughter the feelings themselves had been distorted, as a tree is distorted when the roots are gnawed away, the finest, the most delicate of them, those that suck life into us. She had lost the holiest, the most priceless – and yet she was not dead, must feign life.

He loved her for it. Because in her there was a want, which he recognized. How easy it was to see what would save them. Inwardly, each of them was a cry for love. But they did not hear each other. Perhaps she never understood that he loved her. And he never really believed that she loved him. Their love was like an instrument without strings. An instrument whose tone could have sounded full and deep, though perhaps dark. But the first thing they did when they met was pull the strings off it. The sound still jarred in their ears, they could well remember it.

Such they were. And with their stay here in this house – which was desolate although they lived in it – their life together began, the emptiest and dreariest which two people, who nonetheless must be said to love each other, could offer to share with each other. With that their wandering began, nearly always to remote places where they knew no one. Flee from people, live lonely, like two lovers – and leave each other lonely. Two who wanted to live in loneliness together, the real loneliness, where one is absolutely on one's own.

In the winter they went far north, as if they were not already freezing. It was by a fjord and the house lay close to the water, they lived in the upper storey, which was usually rented out in the summer, in the winter it was cold, with icy windows that never thawed. For the first weeks the dense mist drifting in from the sea lay impenetrably all around, hid everything there. It was a whole world, without things. But it moved, like spirits, formless beings gliding into and through each other. They saw nothing else, did not know where they were. Down under the haze they heard the drift-ice grinding, like murmuring voices from the deep and like jaws biting into each other – like the spirits' conglomerated bodies over which the soul brooded, gliding and gliding without finding rest.

It was not until one morning when the mist was gone that they saw how they were living. The mountains rose blindingly white, like monuments to the blessed, the waters lay covered with snow, shimmering valleys of peace. Everything had become motionless, the whole land lay in an ecstatic rest, clean and still, radiant with death. And the sun poured over it.

Come, my beloved, let us walk out in the sky, in the blessed space where we live. Let us walk in the wide light, in the fields of glittering stars. Behold, the earth is no more. Behold, everything is clear and still, stillness is all, it exists in itself. Let us step into our dwelling of nothing, of heaven's blue hours that open the space they close. Behold, everything is nothing. Everything is only a moment, an hour of eternity that pauses for us to find ourselves in it. Come, my beloved, let us be.

And they walked out into the glittering snow, up on the mountains, down in the valleys, as if without effort, without weight, happy and still, like two of the dead. In the whiteness of all, their senses were annulled, in the streaming light everything became one. They rose to the heights as if without climbing upwards, they wandered down in the valleys as if on a sunny noonday hilltop. Nothing shifting, or changed by life, as in a world. All lay motionless. All was a mere moment.

So long as they could, they stayed in this, until they had to start living again. But for long after they still felt the same untouched calm, the same freedom, the same sense of not being weighed upon by anything. They were neither joyful nor sad. And they did not hem each other in, they could talk together about anything they liked. Something strange and complete settled over them, something inexplicable.

Around them the fields glittered, the woods were veiled in radiance, everything was adorned as for a wedding-feast.

As they were walking a few flakes floated down from the sky, from an almost imperceptible cloud, sank like a gleam through the light, without shading the sun. It was a miraculous sight, light and joyful, happiness itself, free from its earthly weight. And the flakes fell on Hilde's hair and lay there, her bright face glowed with youth and coolness – he had to stop and look at how beautiful it was.

He happened to think of something and he said it. At his mother's wedding it had snowed on her bridal crown, as on Hilde now. That meant good luck. He realized just now that that was what it must mean, must really be.

‘Oh?’ she said. And he recognized the tone in which she always responded if he mentioned anything about his home. For to her that was in some way hateful. He seldom talked about his home and did not in fact think much about it himself, as if he were reluctant to – how long he had felt this he did not really know, probably for a long time. Anyway, he was thinking about his home now.

‘It worked out for them too,’ he continued. ‘Their life was completely happy.’

‘How do you know that?’ she replied.

She seemed to grudge both that they were happy and that he should think so. He thought the fact of their happiness was quite certain, something he did not need to doubt, something firm and true within him, like nothing else there. And the thought flitted through his mind, darkly and half perceived, that even if that were not true then he would still have to believe it. That real love did exist. He felt this without explaining to himself why. He was still far from able to come to grips with this, the idea of compulsion, of being compelled to believe something. He did not even know where this notion came from.

Everything was changed. They had begun to live again. They began talking about love. Which they could not do without tearing everything up – the wounds were wide open again, gaping, and still unable to bleed, for neither would let the other see such a thing. If it had been a struggle in the outer sense, such as struggles between lovers ought to be, so that we can escape from the spiritual side of it, then the snow around them would have been bloody and at last perhaps they would have felt satisfied and tired-out. But it never came to an end. It had to be hidden, everything that mattered was hidden. The same words that cried out of pain tried to muffle it in.

When he saw how she tried to drag down everything for them, as always happened, when he felt all this renewed rawness and humiliation, he lost his way in it.

'No – ' he burst out in a rage, 'where would you learn to love? You were born without a mother. You were bred up by monsters.'

'If you have learnt how to love,' she answered, 'do you love me?'

He answered nothing. For he did not know if he loved her, not now. He did know he hated her – constantly.

Why should he be going here with her when she infected the air, dirtied the entire surrounding world? The whole sky might be open but it was impossible to breathe. Everything they stepped in became clinging mud. How could he endure that?

And so they separated, went their different ways.

He wandered for a long time, disturbed in a way he was accustomed to, as if life should be like that, somehow he did not suffer from it, it had become for him a kind of peace. He went past a village and up among the mountains again. There it was still almost as clear and sunny, although the beams were at a lower angle. On the way home the snow began. That made him calmer because watching the flakes falling always gives a certain restfulness. He stood watching those butterfly souls floating down from the sky, unwritten messages, greetings which hardly came as far as a sigh. Everything felt so still.

When his mother was young, nothing for her had been more beautiful than the snowflakes, big like those he saw now, falling to earth, floating down. She often said so. And he really thought he saw her as a young fair-haired girl standing at the window at home on the farm, behind the geraniums, looking out, watching the flakes coming down over the fields, over the marshes. But, he always added, she could not think that way any longer. Now she always thought what extra drudgery it was for Father, with all this snow. And that was true, they had to keep the whole station clear, they could shovel for whole days on end, long into the evenings. Father never came home so worn out as when there was snow. He well remembered that. And the sharp stick Father kept in his boot-leg, for cleaning the points. No, she could no longer rejoice over the snowflakes.

He did not really know why he came to think about that. His thoughts did not ofter turn back, to home. When they did, he would ask why. And he did not know why it should stab him like this, why it should hurt.

He stood there looking up into the space that opened itself so floating and still. The flakes fell on his face so that it was wet as if someone had wept on it. It felt so mild, so strangely relieving, for he was not able to weep.